HOT GAY EROTICA

HOT GAY EROTICA

EDITED BY RICHARD LABONTÉ

CLEIS
PRESS

Published in the United States by Cleis Press Inc., P.O. Box 14697, San Francisco, California 94114.

Printed in the United States.
Cover design: Scott Idleman
Cover photograph: Jackson Photografix
Text design: Frank Wiedemann
Cleis logo art: Juana Alicia
First Edition.
10 9 8 7 6 5 4 3 2 1

"Be Careful What You Ask For" © 2005 by Nick Alexander, excerpted with permission from *Sottopassaggio* (BIGfib Books, 2005). "The Second Date" © 2005 by Jonathan Asche, first appeared in *Honcho*, October 2005. "Lonesome for October" © 2005 by Steve Berman, first appeared in *X-Factor*. "The Shift" © 2005 by Joe Birdsong. "The Guy in the House" © 2005 by Kal Cobalt, first appeared in *S.M.U.T. Magazine*, April 2005. "Batboy" © 2006 by Jaime Cortez. "A Pardoner's Tale" © 2005 by Wayne Courtois, excerpted with permission from *A Pardoner's Tale,* first appeared in longer form in *Velvet Mafia*, issue 14. "Rude Awakening" © 2006 by Doug Harrison. "You've Heard of It" © 2005 by Vincent Kovar, first appeared online in *Blithe House Quarterly*, Spring 2005. "Wasabi" © 2006 by David May. "Back and Forward" © 2006 by Syd McGinley. "Knives and Roses" © 2005 by Sean Meriwether, reprinted with permission from *Skin & Ink*, edited by Jim Gladstone (Alyson Books, 2005). "The Competitor" © 2005 by Scott Pomfret, first appeared in *Playguy*, June 2005. "Ring Tones" © 2006 by C. B. Potts. "Argentina" © 2006 by Richard Reitsma. "Slips" © 2005 by Rob Stephenson. "Delta Boys" © 2005 by Cat Tailor, first appeared online at twobigmeanies.com, February 2005. "The End" © 2005 by James Williams, first appeared online in *Velvet Mafia*, issue 12, and also appears in *Best American Erotica 2006*, edited by Susie Bright (Simon & Schuster).

For Asa, always Hot

Contents

INTRODUCTION

How many elements of Hot can one collection contain? Quite a range.

Hot can be erotic and amusing—as in Nick Alexander's comic narrative about a man's quirky evening with a pair of leather queens with a penchant for peach; as in Jaime Cortez's generation-gap pickup of a street-smart pussyboy; as in Vincent Kovar's cocked-eye account of an encounter with a persistent porn star; as in Cat Tailor's lusty tale recounting the one-for-all, all-for-one fucking of a quartet of military buddies; as in Steve Berman's fantasy about a calendar boy who comes to life.

Hot can be erotic and unsettling—as in Wayne Courtois's novel excerpt that puts the gay back into ex-gay; as in Richard Reitsma's gripping story about a man reliving the exquisite horror of torture; as in Sean Meriwether's horror-tinged story of the scars that blossom from a barroom assault; as in Doug Harrison's perceptive remembrance of his first sexual experience.

Hot can be erotic and romantic—as in David May's sweet

story about the sixty-year-old who gets the sex and the affection he deserves for his birthday; as in Syd McGinley's brawny story about a closeted rugby player accepting queer love.

Hot can be erotic and lyrical—as in Joe Birdsong's spiritual memory piece about finding transcendence as a fill-in go-go dancer; as in Rob Stephenson's precise exploration of the fetishes that imprint us; as in James Williams's exquisite story about physical magnificence, and lust and love.

And hot can be just plain Hot—as in Jonathan Asche's story about a second date that ends on a cruisy bathroom floor; as in C. B. Potts's story about a Daddy who lets his phone ring while he's servicing the Sir he needs; as in Scott Pomfret's story about bringing a young hunk home from the gym; as in Kal Cobalt's story about the sinister house on the block where all the boys go for sexual satiation.

Hot and Gay and Erotic: a sizzling combo.

Richard Labonté
Perth, Ontario
February 2006

THE GUY IN THE HOUSE

Kal Cobalt

Thomas, the guy in the house, lived toward the end of a
sleepy street of two-stories, in the kind of tree-laden, perfectly paved neighborhood you'd expect to see kids biking
through on their way home from school. Two blocks before
his house, the heavy scent of the trees settled down like fog,
thick from their drooping limbs studded with new buds. It was
Sunday afternoon, and in this town, you could tell; half a dozen
cars passed by me, slow as trains, in gunmetal gray and elderly
white, Pontiacs and Bonnevilles. Newer, smaller cars stayed
home on Sundays here.

Nobody I knew cared about his last name. Mike had told
me about him; Mike said everybody knew about Thomas, the
guy in the house, though Mike was the only one I'd ever heard
talk about him. He gave me the address and told me to go there
Sunday afternoon: "Tell him Mike sent you." I went that Sunday, and every Sunday after, all through the spring. Summer

threatened now, the air swelling with it, and still I made the pilgrimage down the rolled-up sidewalks of the main drag every Sunday without fail, down through the shade of the oaks.

The house didn't look out of place on its street. It was a modest two-story like all the others, with four broad steps up to a little porch where Thomas kept a blue nylon folding camp chair I'd never seen him use and a stack of paperbacks beside it that never seemed to change. He kept all the windows uncurtained and they always seemed dark, a series of gaping mouths set in gray shingles.

He'd left the front door open, the screen door's latch lax but just enough to keep it from swinging open in the breeze. I let myself in, waiting for my eyes to adjust to the dimmer surroundings of the foyer. "Thomas?" I called.

"Hey." He came down the ancient creaking stairs toward me; inside, no amount of maintenance could hide the fact that the house was aged and failing. Thomas was bottle-blond, with a constant ironic smile and dangerous eyes. I always tried not to look too hard at the tattoos that covered half his skin. Looking too hard made them move.

"Hey," I replied. I'd never figured out how he could keep the windows wide open and still end up with so much darkness. Entering the house was like being swallowed.

"You wanna come up?" he asked, stopping on the last stair before the floor.

"Yeah." I stepped close, but he didn't move, didn't turn to move back up the stairs and give me space to follow. I edged to the close side of the stairs, stepping up, and he pressed me gently up against the wall.

"Let's start here," he murmured, tugging the tongue of my belt free of the buckle.

"Okay," I replied, holding my hands out to my sides. I'd

learned the first time not to help him. Thomas always knew exactly what he was doing.

He tugged my jeans and briefs down to my knees, immediately fitting one hand around my cock and cupping the other under my balls. I heard my breathing deepen, returned to my ears by the house's acoustics. Everything sounded amplified within the house's aging walls.

He slipped his hands around my cock and balls without rhythm, just feeling me, squeezing me, until my cock stood out hard and tight. He'd learned the third time I came here that he could milk precum out of me, and as he rested his hand firmly against the base of my cock, getting to his knees, I let out a sharp moan of anticipation. He squeezed the base of my cock, just shy of hard enough to hurt, then moved his hand up toward the head an inch and squeezed again. An inch, another squeeze, an inch, another squeeze, and then he squeezed the head of my cock with thumb and forefinger, pressing a drop of clear fluid from my slit. He watched the fluid slide down the head, waited till it reached the bottom edge of the ridge and was nearly ready to drop to the floor before he licked it up, drawing his tongue wide and flat up over my slit, massaging it firmly.

"Fuck," I whispered, shuddering. Last week he'd made me come just from the slow repetition of milking me and licking me afterward a dozen times.

His hand fitted around the base of my shaft again. Squeeze, squeeze, squeeze, squeeze, and then the knowing press of his fingers. There was more this time, and he waited longer, letting the drip hang off my cock for nearly an inch before he licked it up, spreading it around the head of my cock with his tongue. I pressed my hands against the wall behind me, my sweaty palms flat against the cool wallpaper, and tried to breathe.

Squeeze, squeeze, squeeze, squeeze. He waited, watching the

head of my cock carefully, and when he pressed I had to close my eyes. His tongue was quick this time, light, barely stroking my skin.

He cradled my balls then, already tucked up tight against my shaft, and worked his thumb between them in a slow rub. I opened my eyes, watching him watch my cock, and felt my balls slowly relax under his touch. He took his time, waiting until I could breathe again, and got to his feet. "C'mon," he said simply, and I tugged my jeans up far enough to navigate the stairs properly as I followed.

We went into the only bedroom of the house I'd ever been in. I wondered sometimes if it was the bedroom he used for everyone who came here. It was quaint, like the rest of the house, with a full bed and not much else. He sat me down on the foot of the bed and pulled my jeans down again, this time all the way to my ankles, and took the head of my cock in his mouth and my balls in his hand.

It was always Thomas's hands and mouth, nothing more. Sometimes I thought he might consider his hands and his mouth his most useful tools; sometimes I thought he saved the rest for others, people who didn't call him the guy in the house.

He suckled the head of my cock with rhythmic little pulls, his lips firmly sealed just past the ridge, his tongue cupped up against the underside. He could have made me come in moments—but putting that off was the point of using his hands; his fingers rubbed and massaged and lightly pulled in perfect counter-rhythm, forcing my balls down too far for orgasm to tickle them. I planted my hands on the bed and tried hard not to press my thighs against him, tried to let him do what he wanted. My balls were starting to ache from the play. My cock jumped in his mouth.

He let go of my sack and wrapped his hand around my cock,

high up, almost touching his lips. He rested the pad of his thumb against the underside, just before the ridge, and kept up the tiny wet nursing motion of his mouth. I let out a hoarse groan, close, so close, the heat of his hand around my shaft and his mouth and tongue perfect-wet-tight, and he pressed his thumb in firmly. I gave a sharp, startled cry as something like orgasm shuddered through me, strong enough to leave my fingers and toes numb but different enough for me to know I still hadn't come.

Thomas pulled off, blowing cool air over the head of my cock, which was a deep purple-red now, and went back to massaging my balls down. I couldn't form words, and wouldn't have known what to say if I could; it was a terrifying, painful, perfect torment.

He fit his lips around my cock again, hand around the shaft, thumb at the spot on the underside, and this time I couldn't hold back. I grabbed his shoulder and squeezed tight, my fingers digging into bone as he nursed me up into that same dry shudder again, so close but not there, so good but not good enough. Again he pulled off, again he massaged me down from the edge, and I felt like begging and thanking him all at once.

It felt like a long time that he massaged me. It went from painful to almost pleasant; my cock lost its rock-hard discomfort. The ache was bearable. He angled my cock up a little, enough that I could see the slit, and squeezed the base. Then up a little further.

Oh, God.

Squeeze. Squeeze. Then the press, slow and careful and deliberate, and this time it wasn't just a drop. He let up for a moment and pressed the head again, angling my cock up just a little farther, and precum dribbled back over the top of the head, dripping warm and slow down to my pubic hair. I realized I was making small, desperate groans with every exhale.

Back to the base. Squeeze, squeeze, squeeze, squeeze, each one slower than the last, tighter. A series of three slow presses with thumb and forefinger. I could barely keep my eyes open. There was precum all over his fingers, glistening over the purple head of my cock, slick and clear all over my shaft.

Back to the base. I cried out at the thought of going through the process again. I couldn't breathe. Sweat stuck the front of my T-shirt to my sternum. Thomas's chest was warm between my knees.

Squeeze. I let out a sharp bark, my hands clenching into fists in the bedcovers.

Squeeze. A sob this time, my head falling back.

Squeeze: slower, tighter. I sucked in a breath and held it.

Squeeze and hold, hold, hold. My entire body felt tight as a wire, trembling.

Pad of thumb and forefinger at the head and a series of short, fast presses, and Thomas's mouth fitted around the very tip of my cock, sucking the precum out as he milked it from me, small quick presses, small quick sucks.

I came.

My feet lifted up off the floor and my head came forward, both my hands buried in Thomas's short hair and holding him there, my hips jerking upward uncontrollably as my cock jerked and rocked, cum spilling past Thomas's lips and dripping back over my cock in milky rivulets mixed with his spit. His tongue still flicked at my slit, sucked at it, drawing out jet after jet as I shuddered and shouted.

I came back to myself curled around him, both arms tight around the back of his head, knees digging into his arms. Panting, I let him go, leaning back against the bed, and he slowly began to lick me clean. Dazed, I tipped my head down to watch, unsure I could handle any more. He held my thick, softening cock gently in one hand, moving it this way and that as he began at the base and licked me thoroughly clean with broad, flat strokes not quite sharp enough to make me shudder. When he only had the head left to do, he held my shaft firmly and sank his mouth down on it, forcing a single sharp jerk from me before he pulled away, letting go of me.

"Jesus," I whispered, reaching down to squeeze my cock myself, just to remember what it felt like to touch it, to be in control of it.

Thomas smiled, wiping his mouth and sitting back on his heels. It took me a few minutes to be sure I could take the stairs without falling over.

I retreated to my neighborhood café to recover. The same boy always waited on me: five-ten, brown-haired, tight jeans hidden by his barista apron. He always looked at me more often than he had to, and looked longer than he should. He nodded to me as I came in, and I took my customary seat. A few minutes later, as he brought my trademark caramel macchiato, easy on the ice, I beckoned him closer. "Hey. What's your name?"

"Tim."

"Tim. You ever heard of Thomas, the guy in the house?"

THE COMPETITOR

Scott Pomfret

This is the kid at the gym: He wears baggy basketball shorts that go beyond his knees. Tight, plain white T-shirt. A ratty wool cap half over his eyes like he was dressing as Eminem for Halloween.

He's on the decline bench, working with dumbbells. He's got smooth white arms. Perfect chest with just enough meat on the pecs. He's cross-eyed from the effort, his lips in a little pout. Every time he lowers the weights, his shirt pulls away from his shorts. You get a glimpse of flat, hard belly, a band of underwear stretched on two hard pelvic bones that point at the prize beneath his shorts.

His eyes are hooded, vulnerable. He looks away, he won't catch your eye. But every once in a while, you feel a hot sun burning down on you. You see him in the mirror, checking you out. Not so much checking you out as eating you up. Every last bit. Every drop. Never knew a person could make you feel so naked without your taking off a stitch of clothes. Your heart jumps. Your crotch stirs.

This game goes on for a week. Maybe he's new at the college up on the hill. Maybe he works at one of the kiosks downtown and this is where he comes after dark. The shirts he wears are all a little worn in the back. You can see a hint of pale white skin—sexy vulnerability. You think: *This guy should be easy, he wants it so bad.*

You time your workouts to catch him. You learn his schedule: chest and arms Mondays and Thursdays, shoulders and back Tuesdays and Fridays. You wonder: *When does he work that fine ass? That pert little shelf that his b-ball shorts hang on?*

Most times you think he's not conscious of you. He goes through his whole workout head down and sullen. You're about to give up hope for the day when suddenly, he catches your eye. He's one of those boys who seems unconscious of you, then suddenly turns and flashes a warm penetrating look and holds it, like the two of you were in on some private joke, even though you've never met him before.

Usually he comes and goes without doing much more than hanging a jacket in the locker room. But then about two weeks after you've set eyes on him, he has a full bag slung over his shoulder when he saunters into the gym. You time it right: after the workout, when he goes toward the locker room, you give him exactly two minutes by the wall clock, then follow him in.

The locker room is almost deserted. One or two big-belly guys are straightening their ties or blowing dry what's left of their hair. The shower is running. You flick off your gym shorts like they were a distraction. You grab a towel. Cinch it over your waist.

He's the only one in there. He hasn't bothered to pull shut

the curtain of his stall. His dark hair is plastered against his skull. His eyes are closed. The water streams over his face. His back is firm, not too soft, not an inch of extra skin at his waist, which is narrow as a boy's. He's pale, almost blue-veined, and thinner than you thought, which only makes the pertness of that rounded mound of ass all the more adorable.

The water splashes off his shoulders. You wish you could catch it on your tongue, and lap that kid up. His crotch hair is also plastered to his skin. His cock is rigid, up-angled in that won't-quit, young-guy way. As you watch, he soaps his hand and grabs himself, squeezing his buttcheeks. He presses his cock into the little tube he has made from his palm. His jaw hangs open like he's made himself stupid with pleasure. The water gushes in and out. He makes a little snorting noise, and puts his other hand against the wall like he needs to catch his balance.

He strokes his soap-slicked dick, and now it's you that feels like you're getting dizzy. His nipples are hard despite the heat. The muscles of his belly alternately clench and release, a perfect little six-pack. His thighs tense, and the water runs down into his crotch and disappears just where you would like to put your face. You are struck dumb and staring.

You suddenly feel a warmth on your face, on your bare skin. His lazy brown eyes are on you, all over you, passing from pecs to hips, lifting your towel. His eyes gleam. His lashes are long and caught with dewdrops. You wait for scorn to pass over his face now that he's caught you looking, but the look you see is more relief, ecstasy, relaxation. You realize that you are the object of the kid's masturbatory fantasies. He's been jerking off to you for the last two weeks.

With a snap of your finger, you loosen the towel. There's a moment before it slides loose when it catches on your cock, which is large, engorged. Your cock twitches and the towel drops. The kid's eyes go wide, he stumbles a little in the shower cubicle and his strokes get faster. His eyes are fixed below your waistline.

You take a quick look over your shoulder for witnesses. Then you slip into the shower stall next to him. The stall smells goatlike with hormones and young-man sweat. You run your hands down the kid's smooth skin. Those well-worked shoulders and lats. You raise his arms above his head, and sidle in behind him. You lean against his backside, your cock now straight up, lodged between his meaty asscheeks, but not inside, nowhere near that.

You put your arms around him and pull him back against you. There's strong resistance, and his muscles tense. You pass your hands over his chest, slide down over soap-greased abs. He jumps when your fingertips hit the treasure trail, faint as it is, and then slide down, following instinct. The shower water pours over your ears, making a disorienting seashell sound. You soap your own hand. You stroke him off. You are surprised by the size of the cock on such a slim man. It is hot to the touch, hotter than seems possible. You stroke once, twice, three times. He moans, grabs your forearms for dear life, forces his butt back against you.

Then suddenly he bucks, the penis head swells, and he spurts once, twice, more, white cascades that spatter the stall and are only slowly washed down by the shower. The jizz is slicked over your fingers. You bring your hand to your face. You smell the mix of soap and spunk, a heady, dirty mix that always reminds you of clean young hot men.

For a second the kid lolls against you like a rag doll, then he starts up. He hears again the voices of the big-belly men around the corner in the locker room who talk about their children. The kid jumps out of your embrace, jumps a clear five feet from you in one bound. He snatches his towel from the rack. He hurries toward the lockers like he is embarrassed. His pace is electric, his body is stiff and self-conscious, then becomes slinky, as if he'd like to disappear entirely.

You think: *Shit, I've scared him off.* You are disappointed and rock hard and have a handful of jizz not your own swiftly getting cold. Then, just as you are about to lose sight of him, just as he reaches the threshold where he's going to turn the corner toward the lockers, he looks back over his shoulder. He stops for the briefest infinitesimal second, towel hanging by his side, chest puffed up with something like pride. And he smiles back at you, shyly. It's a world of teeth and whiteness and great big puppy dog eyes. And there's an edge to it, like only an athlete can have. A competitor.

As you expect, he waits for you. He sees you just before you see him, so he moves away from the door to the gym, down the sidewalk. He walks tough, but with a lilt, with grace; a little belligerent, a little shy, like he came from a tough neighborhood and doesn't know how to fit in where the homes are nice. You walk fast. You're close, but not too much; not breathless, cool or predatory.

"Yo," you say.

He turns, not surprised. He flashes you that white-hot look, then looks away. He bites his lower lip. He slings his bag on his shoulder a little tighter though it has not slipped.

"Yeah?" he says.

"Where you headed? Dorm?"

He shrugs and nods.

"Got your own room?"

He looks pained. "No, man. My roommate, you know."

"Why don't you come hang with me? My place?"

"Now?"

You nod. For a moment, the kid's torn. His eyes skitter this way and that like squirrels chasing each other around a park. He shifts weight from one foot to the other, you see his cock move in his gym shorts and realize he's wearing no underwear. He looks off into a distance so full of promise and things to think about you can hardly imagine. Then he grins. He looks down, embarrassed.

He says, "Okay, man."

You walk side by side to your place. Every once in a while your arms brush and he jumps away, and the hair rises on your forearm and the back of your neck, and the shock seems to make him talkative.

He says, "Back there…"

"Yeah?"

"I was thinking about you, when…you know. I touched myself."

"I know."

"You do?"

He grows visibly scared at being so obvious.

You say, "It was written all over your face."

He looks abashed, shuts up. Then he's curious, then he's mean. He opens his mouth to say something. You push him into an alcove in the building you're walking past. You kiss him hard, your tongue in his mouth. He's too startled to fight back, then he joins in. You are looking at him eye to eye; for the longest time he looks at you, as you explore every bit of his mouth with your tongue and taste his sweet hot young breath that comes in gasps.

Then he shoves you away, backhands his mouth, looks up and down the street and says, "We got to be cool."

"That *was* cool," you say. "Way cool. I couldn't help myself. You're hot."

He blushes, but he knows he's hot. Still, it gives him a boost to have you say it aloud. It makes him stand tall, his pride makes him even hotter. Cocky, the way you like them.

You've hardly shut the door to your apartment when his bag drops like a bowling ball. There's nothing cool about him. He rushes at you, throws himself on to you like a koala in heat. He tugs your shirt up and off, capturing and pinning your arms; bites your nipple; struggles with your belt loop. He's all over you, frantic as a motherfucker.

You force him back against the door. You put your head close to his, you jam your tongue down his throat. He is fumbling with his own shorts and shirt. They come off his slim body like sheets, no fat to catch on. His shorts snag on his right ankle. He's still got the wool cap on and nothing else, gold chain around his neck, big studded cross stark metal against fleshy chest.

You push him over on the sofa. He seems to resist you as he sits down. You put your mouth in his crotch. Force aside his legs. Cup his nuts with your hand. It hasn't been more than twenty minutes since he blew his load in the gym, but already he's hot and hard and good to go. You flick your tongue at the tip of his cock. You run down one side of the shaft to the base and back, using just the tip of your tongue. You blow cool air, and every breath makes his cock jump.

You can't resist a look. As you play his cock with your tongue you look up. He's splayed back watching you suck him off. Like he can hardly believe it. His hands are gripped at each side as if he is going to start doing dips on your couch, or vault you toward the door.

You lift his feet from the ground and put his ankles over your shoulders. You duck your head under his nuts, and begin to eat the base of his shaft below the nuts. Forcing your teeth against it, where it runs under his pelvis toward the ass. You put your mouth around a nut, which makes him nervous; you feel the thrill run through his body. Then you work back up his cock from the base to the tip, nibbling, dragging your teeth lightly as you take the whole shaft into your mouth. The kid likes to feel it hard when he's given head. He moans, and already his nuts rise up and his cock swells.

So you stop.

His eyes pop open.

"Why're you stopping? I'm close."

"Too close," you say. You grin. You stand up. Tear off your pants. Throw your shirt over his face. He pulls it off, throws it to the side, annoyed. He starts to stand. You push him back on the sofa. Kick the ottoman out of the way.

"My turn," you say. You plan to feed your cock to that fine wet mouth. Imagine tracing his lips with the head of your penis. Imagine him open wide, choking your manhood down, grateful and meek.

He bites his lip. He dodges and slips away. He circles you, bare naked, one foot forward, one back, thighs tensed. You turn to face him. He feints twice, and then strikes as suddenly as a snake. He seizes your wrists with those talon hands, calloused from his workout. You drop to your knees and try to get under his body and boost him off his legs. Lightning quick, he kicks his legs out behind himself where you can't reach. He clasps your neck and you wriggle free, breaking his grip. You rush him. You knock heads. You toss each other this way and that. First on the sofa. Then on the ottoman, which rolls off to the other side of the room. Someone's ankle gets trapped in a light cord; a lamp falls from the side table and flashes blue.

He's a wiry, quick motherfucker, but eventually your greater strength and bulk win out. You get him facedown on the carpet, pert ass up, pinned. He won't give up. You press his face to the floor. You hiss in his ear, bite at his lobes, press your stubbled cheek to his smooth face. He struggles, then realizes it's futile with your weight on top of him. You lie against him. His skin is hot to the touch. You both catch your breath. You kiss the back of his neck, lick up the sweat that beads on his hairline.

You work down from his neck between his shoulder blades. His back is smooth and unblemished with two hard ropes of muscle down each side of the spine, guiding you toward his ass. He has now relaxed, given up the struggle. He stiffens when your mouth reaches his ass. You guess he has never had his ass eaten out.

You plunge in ferociously, pulling apart his cheeks, exposing the pink dark hole. You lap and fill your mouth, nose and throat with that clean, assy smell, that copper taste. There are just a couple of hairs you slick aside. You suck your fingers, wet them thoroughly, and slide one in, just a fingertip.

He looks at you for reassurance. "You'll let me do that to you, too?"

"Sure," you say. You'd say anything. But your words relax him and he draws your finger in with the muscles of his rectum. He is tight and strong and firm, as if he worked out with these muscles as well.

"Mmmm," he says, like he's smelled home cooking.

You boost him up to the sofa and roll him on his side. You locate a stash of lube and condoms in the drawer on the side table. You lift his leg a little, lube his ass. Your finger slides easy now, and there is no resistance; he is watching you insert your finger in him, he winces and then gasps open. You slide the condom over your cock, he watches, he looks like he wants to help; you put lube in his hand and he slicks your covered cock with his palm. You lift his leg and fuck him sideways. Slowly. The muscles of his chest tremble, shiver with apprehension. Then you can look at nothing but where your cock enters his firm gym-body, peach-fuzz ass. In and out, the first electric thrills starting deep down in your body, along your spinal cord, and rising up until you lose control of your hips and thrust so deeply into his slim body you think he might burst. He tightens his sphincter slightly, a little wink, and you explode and convulse, pouring into him all your soul and knowledge and experience.

He gets himself off with his hand while you are still inside him, flecking white cum all over the sofa. He's staring back at you, not for a second letting go of your gaze, like he's got just a little time to commit you to memory. He's a defiant little fuck, his wool hat slightly askew, necklace shining bright, brown eyes hard and dark like he's just figured out the rules but for sure is going to become quite the little player.

WASABI

David May

*Love is a thing that's too serious to be joked about,
and too absurd to be taken seriously....*
—Lytton Strachey

D on still lived in the house he had inherited from his grand-
parents some thirty years ago. For twenty of those years, it
had been the site of countless drugged parties and all-night or-
gies, parties that came to a sudden stop in the 1980s. The house
was on Capital Hill, large, barn shaped, and pleasant, but need-
ing refurbishment when fate designated that Don be among the
first of the tribe to settle and rebuild in the neighborhood. On
learning later that his homesteading had made him an example
to other men loving men and a role model to the next genera-
tion, he felt obligated to settle down to a series of long-term,
nonmonogamous relationships that each ended in friendship.

With every spouse he painted the house a different color:

First there was Alex and the safe neutral taupe that succumbed to the bright buttercup yellow that Doug had wanted. Then with Ted (who was known to purge half his wardrobe each time the color of the moment shifted) it shifted to a too precious mauve, which in its turn was altered by Don to that soft shade of green, somewhere between moss and sage, peculiar to the Pacific Northwest. By pure good fortune, Don and the house had been spared teal.

As he approached his sixtieth birthday (which he had been preparing for by never referring to his actual age but rather to what his age would be come October), Don basked in the knowledge that his life was a good one. He socialized often with his numerous friends (so many former lovers), taught English at the community college (where each autumn brought some new beautiful boy, sweet and sincere and growing his first beard, oblivious to his own beauty or how much pain it caused Don), entertained whenever he pleased (which was at least weekly), and delighted in his favorite niece's family gossip on her frequent visits. His neighbors thought him something of an eccentric as he puttered about in his garden wearing a wide-brimmed hat (purchased in the Cotswolds because it looked like something Lytton Strachey might've worn while gardening). The neighbors smiled to each other knowingly, feeling liberal and tolerant (and unnecessarily proud of being both), never imagining that Don routinely received some of the most sordid bareback pornography in his mailbox.

Pornography, in fact, was his primary release. Occasionally there was a meeting of eyes on Broadway that led to a quick tumble that was never repeated; or the rare trip to Basic Plumbing when he absolutely had to have a warm, wet mouth wrapped around his fat dick. Most often, though, he jerked off to images of leather-clad, hairy, bearded men fucking like banshees. He made a weekly date with himself, taking his hard-on pill first to ensure the hardest possible cock, and thus the intensity of the orgasm—for he could still, if the moon and stars were right, shoot over his shoulder, though now with only a single shot that left Don and his balls satisfied, if drained, for days.

Having had the body type fashionable during his youth—lean and sinewy rather than beefy and buff, as was the current fashion—he had had more than his share of lovers. His dark lush mustache and wavy black hair made his otherwise plain, if overlarge, features almost handsome, even causing tricks to compare him to a popular TV detective. Now the thinning hair was cut short, and, like the mustache, more salt than pepper. Having hiked, run or jogged, done aerobics, or lifted weights for most of the last four decades, he managed to maintain a solidness of build unusual in his peers, but then he had never been heavy a day in his life, nor able to achieve the massive muscularity he had admired in each of his husbands.

In addition to a firm body, Don had also been blessed with an enormous cock, something that caused him to be continually cast as a top, even back when the sexual politics of the day demanded an egalitarian exchange of positions. Bottoms, of which there were always more, never demanded he roll over for them, but rather that he rest until ready for another round. Content with the pleasure he brought to so many, Don rarely attempted to reverse the roles, and even more rarely met with success if he tried.

His friends assured him that he looked at least five, if not ten years younger than his fifty-nine years, but Don was acutely aware of being past his prime, perhaps even past being a Hot Daddy. The truth of it was that he was actually handsome now, having finally grown into his features. He was also single, and being single, he was sometimes lonely and horny, and so unsure of himself.

On his fifty-fifth birthday, Don's friends had arranged a party for him at a local bathhouse, half filling it with friends and well-wishers. Don scored brilliantly that night, time after time, with one handsome man after another. He never went back to the baths after that birthday celebration because he knew that the night could never be repeated. Rather than return to the baths and face his fear of feeling foolish and unwanted, he preferred to live with the memory of that one perfect steamy night, to jerk off thinking of it whenever he woke up alone at some odd hour with nothing but his hard dick to ease his loneliness. To go back to the baths might allow the young and beautiful to corral him with the ubiquitous losers that had peopled every bathhouse for as long as could he remember: the soft elderly men wearing flip-flops, the unkempt hippies stinking of patchouli, the morbidly obese cock-suckers, the too skinny sissies, the pimply-faced bag whores, the homely middle-aged men sitting in darkened rooms chain-smoking, the sagging old men wanting to get fucked, the ugly men with big dicks who followed pretty boys down the halls torment-ing their prey with the sound of smacking lips. If his memory was cruel to this clan, fear made him cruel. He had once been among the young and beautiful that had decried these same men as eroti-cally useless. Now his former dismissal of them came back to haunt him as he contemplated the unavoidable reality that some who would once have found him attractive would now discard him to that rubble of men known as: He Used to Be Hot.

Deciding that he wanted something, or at least someone, special for his sixtieth birthday, and certain that he would have to pay for it, he decided to treat himself. He would hire a professional, but not just any local rent boy, of which there were many. He wanted someone to whose image he had masturbated, someone he had imagined (as they used to say) fucking into oblivion: Don wanted one of the gods to descend from Olympus and into his bed. He went online and scanned the appropriate websites looking for the right one, tentatively contacting a few he thought especially attractive. Each man he emailed responded within a day or two, some immediately. When he explained that he was celebrating his sixtieth birthday, most asked to see his picture before committing themselves. Don thought this very unprofessional and dismissed them out of hand, even if he might (as his friends continually assured him) have nothing to hide.

It was only when watching one of his favorite DVDs that it occurred to him to contact his favorite furry butch bottom, a handsome tattooed young man who deserved his sexy *nom de porn*: Tommy Tusker. Here was a man who seemed to thoroughly enjoy his work, who could kiss for hours (even if professionals were said to do everything but kiss when working), and who appeared in every interview to be bright and personable. Best of all, in all his latest photos he had a becoming new beard. Finding Tommy Tusker was easy enough, the Internet providing the trail in seconds. Even more important, he quickly learned from others online that Tommy Tusker had a reputation for being both friendly and reliable. Don sent him a carefully composed email:

> *Dear Tommy Tusker:*
> *I will be celebrating my sixtieth birthday soon and would like to engage your services to help me celebrate living so damn long. I will fly you to Seattle and reserve a nice hotel room downtown for us. In addition to quality time alone, I'm hoping that you will also join me for a birthday dinner, just the two of us, at someplace special. Please let me know if you are available and what kind of deposit you require in addition to airfare. BTW: I really like the new beard*

*and have always thought you were one of the hottest
men on video since Al Parker!*

The answer was almost immediate, and in the affirmative:

Don:
   *Thanks for the compliments! Al Parker? WOW!
   What a nice thing to tell a guy. I'd be honored to help
   you celebrate your birthday and would do my best
   make it special for you. Please remember that what
   you are engaging is only my time. Any activity that
   occurs between us will be negotiated separately on my
   arrival. Seattle is one of my favorite cities and I look
   forward to meeting you. Below are my particulars.*

Don was almost flattered by the promptness, politeness, and
clarity of the correspondence. Airfare was purchased, a limousine and a room with a spectacular view reserved. The day was
more than a month away but Don was already anxious, afraid
of disappointment. A week before the event, however, he received an email to erase his worries:

Don:
   *Just to confirm that I will be with you for your
   birthday next week. Please let me know if there is
   anything special I can do for you by way of preparation or appearance. Below is the itinerary you arranged through my travel agent. Will you meet me at
   the airport?*

Don contemplated Tommy's query as to what he might like, and
answered simply:

*Just please have your beard. A limo will meet you at
the airport. Really looking forward to meeting you.*

His birthday morning found Don happier than any birthday
had found him in years. He taught his class as usual, allowed
friends to take him to lunch, opened the stack of birthday cards
that had been piling up for several days, and reassured his favorite niece that he really did have a date for that night and he
would be happy to see her at the party his friends were giving
him that weekend.

He had pondered what to wear for weeks, even trying several different outfits in front of the mirror as he used to do for a
first date. In the end he wore what he had worn all day: pressed
jeans, a polo shirt, and a tweed blazer. His professor disguise, as
he called it. He checked into the hotel feeling surprisingly calm
and even managed a short nap on the enormous bed before wak-
ing up when room service knocked to deliver the champagne
and canapés that came with the suite.

Less than ten minutes later, there was another knock, and
Don's heart jumped, his calm deserting him. He gave himself a
final glance in the mirror, the habit of so many first dates, before
opening the door.

Tommy Tusker walked in wearing the ubiquitous tight
501s, T-shirt, and leather jacket, a small bag slung over his
shoulder. The uniform may have been perfunctory, but Don
wouldn't have had it any other way. The outfit was popular
because it was sexy and became a man's frame, especially a
hot young man like the one before him extending his hand and
smiling broadly as if genuinely happy to see him.

"Don?"

"Yes," answered Don, shaking the offered hand. "Tommy,
it's good to meet you."

"Likewise. I've been looking forward to this trip since you wrote to me."

He was as handsome as Don had expected, and even sexier than he was on video, if perhaps a bit shorter, though this was hardly a disappointment. His dark hair seemed lighter than on video, as was his beard, but this was incidental.

"Not as much as I have."

"Oh, I don't know," said Tom stepping closer to Don. "I think this is pretty darn special."

He kissed Don fully on the mouth, the softness of his lips and the bristle of the beard providing the contrast that Don found irresistible. Don kissed him back, held him in his arms for several minutes before disengaging, breathless and afraid of rushing too soon into what he was now even more certain was to come. He was perhaps old fashioned in some ways, and on any first date Don liked to take it slow.

"Happy birthday," offered Tommy.

"Thanks. I, that is, I…champagne?"

"Sure. Why don't you sit down and relax. Let me get the champagne."

Don sat on the loveseat facing the floor-to-ceiling window: downtown Seattle, Puget Sound, the Olympic Mountains, and the setting sun were spread before him like a living backdrop. A moment later Tommy was sitting next to him, handing him his champagne, still smiling at him.

"This is nice," said Tommy, looking around. "Nice room, beautiful view, hot Daddy. Thanks for asking me."

"My pleasure, Tommy. You know, you're even handsomer in real life."

Tommy blushed, even broke eye contact a moment, before reaching up to touch Don's face, stroking Don's stubble, as if to say that his touch were the only thanks he could give for the compliment, a gesture so intimate that for a split second Don forgot to breathe.

The sun was setting, and at that instant the very air took on a golden tone, then red-gold, then red, then violet. Neither could speak for several moments as they sat quietly in the shifting light followed by the purple-shadowed dark, both men in awe of the twilight's beauty. Then Don realized that he had his arm around Tommy, that Tommy's head was leaning against his chest as if they had known each other for years, as if what was about to happen was not mere sex, but intimacy. Tommy lifted his face to Don's and Don kissed him again, almost tentatively. This time they let their kisses linger, let their tongues explore each other, let their mouths make friends as they hadn't done before.

Tommy's hands deftly explored Don's body as they kissed, and he murmured his approval on discerning the size and hardness of Don's dick. He slowly undressed Don, kissing his nipples, sucking his cock, and licking his balls as he did. Then he led Don by the hand up the few steps to the bed, sat him down, and turned on a single lamp. Standing beneath that one light Tommy undressed, slowly and teasingly, touching himself as he did, looking at Don and smiling the whole time, promising pleasure and affection and the touch that heals all wounds. He paused in the light, naked and erect, turning this way and that to show off the solidness of his build, the implied strength of his arms, back, and chest. Bending over, then squatting, he displayed his thick, hard legs and magnificent butt.

Done posing, Tommy approached Don and knelt in front of him. Tommy smiled a moment, looking pleased with what he saw, before opening his mouth and taking most of Don's huge cock down his throat with one try. Alternating between a deep-throat and a hand-and-mouth technique that sent shudders up and down Don's spine for what seemed like hours, Tommy got greedy and even gagged on the cock at times, slurping and moaning his appreciation for what he was sucking. Alert to every change in Don's body and demeanor, Tommy knew when Don had danced on the edge long enough. He paused and looked up at Don, still stroking the beautiful fat cock.

"What do you want me to do, Daddy? It's your birthday and you get to call the shots. You've got an awesome Daddy dick. Are you going to fuck me with it? Man, I'd really like that. I bet you'd make me cum buckets if you fucked me. Or do you want to suck my cock for a while? Look how hard it is. You've got me so turned on."

Don pulled Tommy off his knees and kissed him again, guided him over onto the bed and touched him all over, caressed the supple smooth skin, the soft silky hair that covered his muscular chest, torso, butt, and legs. With every kiss he tasted Tommy's youth, his beauty.

"You're so fucking hot I can't stand it," whispered Don. "You're so handsome. I can't believe this is real."

"Fucking hot Daddy. Man, oh man, I'm a lucky boy."

Don tried to delay the inevitable, to keep himself from fucking Tommy too soon. He sucked Tommy's beautiful cock with its coral head dripping salty honey, licked the smooth balls that felt almost as tumescent as his cock. Finally he rolled Tommy over on his stomach and pried the furry melons apart before tasting the finest, pinkest fuckhole Don had ever seen. It was even prettier in person, already moist and glistening, asking for attention. Don dove in head first, tongue extended. The hole opened to him, clean and sweet. Don's nose sniffed the soft hair it was buried in, musky and fine, another aphrodisiac that made his cock ache as it hadn't ached in years, arching upward like a wand in the hand of Merlin, demanding notice. Ever so slowly, Don kissed his way upward, over the smooth muscular back, licking

the black-inked deltoids and traps. All on its own, his cock found
the nest it was looking for, the hot wet pinkness that opened up
to it, that swallowed him even as Tommy gasped in pain.

On hearing Tommy's small cry, Don stopped, waited wordlessly for the nod and sigh that said to go ahead. Don proceeded
slowly, kissing Tommy's neck and ears, all the while whispering
the endearments of a mind clouded by desire: "Oh, baby, oh,
baby. It feels so good. You're so fucking hot. Your butt is so
amazing. Oh, baby, oh, baby..."

Don increased the pace slightly, watching Tommy's profile as
he did, looking for signs of Tommy's pleasure, Tommy's delight
in what was happening inside his body, this merging of men, the
melding of generations, the mixing of bodily juices inside the
cauldron that was Tommy's fuckhole.

Sweat poured off of Don, sweat that formed a slick layer
between the two bodies moving in sync with a shared desire that
was already far past stopping.

"Oh, yeah, Daddy," Tommy whimpered. "Oh, fuck yeah,
Dad. It feels so fucking good. It's so damn big it hurts but it feels
so good. Daddy, Daddy..."

Don had heard these words countless times before, but it
still turned him on, as all men with big dicks are turned on by
the praise of their members. It was nothing new, but the voice
saying the words, Tommy's voice, was young and fresh, manly
and lustful. Aging men might want to see themselves through a
new lover's eyes, but they also want to hear their praises sung
by a new voice, a young voice that echoed their own desires and
banished their fears.

Don fucked Tommy as he knew he had to, twirling Tommy's
body around on his cock, changing positions every few minutes,
making Tommy cry out in pain and pleasure each time Don
shifted Tommy's body to increase their shared joy. Don was

a masterful fuck, always had been, earning a reputation for a prowess and technique that had once produced a well-beaten path to his door. It was all beautifully familiar to Don: the sound of two sweaty bodies slapping together, Tommy's cries of delight, his own moans as he headed toward climax, the smell of man sex permeating the room.

With one of Tommy's legs over his shoulder, with one knee on the bed and his other leg extended behind him, Don was racing toward home when he heard Tommy cry:

"Can I cum, Daddy? Please, Dad? I'm so close."

"Yeah," came Don's voice, so hoarse he almost didn't recognize it. "Yeah, baby. Cum now!"

Tommy's cock arched in the air, and with no hands helping it, spewed lava-hot jizz across their bodies and all over the bed, hitting the headboard and the lampshade where it clung and sizzled in the heat of the bulb. At the same moment, Don roared, flung back his head, arched his body, and shot his wad. They both felt his cock convulse inside of Tommy, felt the ribbons of semen spew deep inside Tommy's body.

Without disengaging, Don collapsed on top of Tommy, whispering incoherently as he waited to catch his breath, as Tommy murmured yet more praise for what had been twenty minutes of transient exultation.

"Oh my fucking god," was all Don could say.

"Hot Daddy," Tommy responded. "Fucking hot Daddy."

They kissed for a few minutes as they felt Don's cock go limp inside Tommy, as it finally withdrew with a small audible pop, as they both felt Don's cum dribbling out of Tommy's fuckhole.

While Tommy showered, Don counted out the money, plus a tip, and put it in an envelope that he laid next to Tommy's leather jacket. Later, after Don had showered and they were ready to go to dinner, Don saw that the envelope had moved to the night table but was still unopened.

At the hotel room, neither had done more than taste the champagne that had eventually gone flat and warm, while the canapés went stale, as they had fucked themselves into oblivion. Now, over wine with dinner at a French bistro near the Market, Tommy chatted easily, talked about his friends and family, answered questions about making videos, and flirted with Don the whole while, never losing eye contact for more than a few seconds at a time. Don thought back to a time at the Folsom Street Fair, ten or more years before, when he'd seen a popular porn star of the day looking bored and annoyed with the small, obsequious man who had obviously paid him for his company that afternoon. Tommy was so different, even holding Don's hand across the table, offering what felt like genuine, if limited, affection.

After dinner, Tommy took Don's hand again as they walked through the steep narrow streets just above the Market

"This has been fun, Dad. Thanks again for inviting me."

"I'm glad you had fun, too. I hope you did, anyway."

"Oh, I've had fun. You saw me cum, didn't you? And that was a great dinner, too. Really great. Good sex, good food, a hot Daddy. Who could ask for more?"

Don wanted to ask if Tommy didn't get taken out a lot, but didn't dare risk shattering the fragile illusion that Tommy was there for any reason other than money. But why was he being so genuinely nice? Don hadn't expected to be kissed, or touched with such tenderness, or even to hear the kind of language, obscene with desire and longing, that he had heard from Tommy. How much was genuine appreciation, if only an appreciation for being appreciated? If Don had treated Tommy like a whore, would he have been offered as much of Tommy's natural geniality and pleasure in another man's touch? Don wanted to think Tommy was responding to his genuine appreciation of him, that Tommy might even enjoy Don's company because of it.

"You've made this birthday a really happy one, Tommy. Thank you."

"Ted. My real name is Ted. I wish you'd call me that."

"Ted. I've always liked that name. One of my lovers was a Ted."

"And you called him your Teddy Bear, right?"

"You know I did."

"All guys named Ted are called Teddy Bear."

"Yes, probably they are, Ted. It will take a little while to get used to your real name. Forgive me if I forget and call you Tommy."

Ted looped his arm through Don's, drawing himself closer for warmth.

"It's cold here. I forget how much colder than San Francisco Seattle is this time of year."

Don hailed a cab and they went back to the hotel. Wanting to prolong the evening, Don suggested a drink in the bar. Don ordered a whisky and Ted asked for a Perrier. The bar was elegant in an overpriced, expensive-hotel kind of way, and sparsely filled. They were the only male couple in the room, making Don feel suddenly very old and very odd, and certain that he was being judged. Who would look at them and not know Ted was being paid? Don downed his whisky and suggested they head back to their room.

They slipped into bed together and Ted, naked and beautiful, cuddled next to him, rubbing Don's chest.

"My butt's sore, but we can do it again if you want. I kind of like getting fucked when my butt is still feeling tender from the last fuck. It turns me on."

"No, that's okay, baby. Dad's tired. Maybe in the morning."
Even as said this, he knew it wouldn't happen: that fuck had
drained him for a day or two to come.

"Goodnight, Dad. Happy birthday."

"Goodnight, baby."

They kissed one last time.

It was only as he drifted off to sleep that Don realized he had
forgotten to take his hard-on pill that afternoon. Tommy's sweet-
ness, even more than this youth, had been better than any pill.

When Don woke up around noon, he was alone. Ted/Tommy
and the envelope of money were gone. On the desk was an au-
tographed studio photo inscribed:

To Daddy Don from his boy Tommy Tucker.

A nice touch, Don thought: a little bonus. He ordered breakfast
from room service and was heading back into the shower when
he noticed that there was also a note on the nightstand:

Dear Don,
*   You were sleeping so soundly and I didn't want*
to wake you. And I hate saying good-bye when I've
had such a good time and really, really like someone
as much I like you. You're such a great guy, such a
hot Daddy, you should be loved by someone 24/7. I
hope you are.
*   Your friend,*
*   Ted*

Don smiled, almost wept, but was in fact not disappointed by
Ted's absence. The morning would've been an anticlimax, a

bitter aftertaste when they finally said good-bye. Ted was wiser than his years, kinder than he needed to be. He hoped Ted's heart would never be too badly bruised, at least not more than was absolutely inevitable.

Since it was yet another beautiful autumn day, and perhaps the last sunny day for months, Don decided to walk, heading up Pike Street toward Capital Hill and home. Happier than he was sad on reaching this time in his life, thinking of all those he had known who never made it to fifty, let along sixty, he embraced his age and the city he called home. For all he knew, he might be the envy of many. Lost in these thoughts, he didn't hear someone call his name until the second, louder, closer call.

"Don! How you doing? Haven't seen you in forever."

It was Ted, the original Ted who had once been Don's lover and insisted they paint the house that too precious mauve. Always cute if a little chunky, and perhaps even a little chunkier now, Ted was still handsome and sporting a mustache again— just like in the old days when all the boys on the Hill were collectively known as clones. Just a year or two younger than Don, Ted still worked part-time as a nurse at Swedish Hospital.

"Ted! I almost didn't recognize you. You're not wearing orange anymore?"

"I never wore orange. It was tangerine. But tangerine is dead to me. Now it's all about wasabi."

Don laughed, delighted as always with Ted's odd combination of seriousness and self-parody.

"Guess what, Ted? I'm sixty! Who would of thought we'd ever live this long?"

"It's like I tell the kids at the hospital, 'Live fast, die young, and leave a beautiful corpse' only sounded like a good idea at the time. How wrong we were."

Ted gave Don a kiss on the mouth.

"Happy birthday, handsome. Sixty is the new forty, you know."

"Really? How so?"

"I read somewhere that fifty was the new thirty, so it just widow stands to reason."

"Of course, Teddy Bear. On your way to work?"

"No, I've done my two shifts for the week. I'm just doing errands."

"Then let me walk with you."

He put his arm over Ted's broad shoulder as they walked past Toys in Babeland, both glancing in the window at all the wares that still titillated them.

"By the way, I was wondering something, Teddy Bear."

"Yes?"

"Tell me, why did we ever break up?"

BATBOY

Jaime Cortez

He's a pussyboy and I can spot it from half a block away. The runway insinuations of his walk. The girly curves in the hips and ass. The big belt, the too-tight jeans flouting the baggy hip-hop style of the neighborhood. He's one of those boys who really should just go ahead and cross-dress, but instead occupies that gender that most fags put in the "major turn-offs" section of their personal ads. I slow down as I pass him. He turns and stares. He smiles tentatively, and I tilt my head slightly. In the rearview mirror, he waves boldly with both arms and torso as I retreat. Ten points for enthusiasm. I flip a U-turn and wait for him in a red zone by a hydrant. As he approaches, I push the switch and lower the passenger window. The rico suavity of this action makes me forget my ride is of the genus "Speckled '86 Bondo Honda." He bends and sticks his head in.

"Hola." He trails the final *a* of the word like the starlets in Mexican wrestling films.

"Hola. Where you going?"

"Ooh, just anywhere."

"Oh yeah? Me too. Wanna ride?"

"Yesss."

He throws his gym bag in the backseat, climbs in, and sits. Whew. CK1 fumigation. Code Blue. I roll down my window and then his for good measure. He would have been a sexy boy if he wanted to play that up, but he didn't. Skin brown and pretty as a girl's. Eyebrows plucked. Hair hennaed up the yin yang, bringing up the red tones in his skin, big lips but parched. As we pull out, he asks, "You live around here?"

"Yeah. Over by Seventeenth and Valencia."

"I bet it's nice, your apartment."

"Wanna come up?"

"Yess."

As I turn onto Valencia, he slides his hand over my crotch.

"Wow," he says, "you're ready to go."

"I can't help it."

"You can do whatever you want with me."

"Like what?"

"Anything."

In my bedroom, he asks to use the bathroom. I gesture to the door. Before entering, he goes to his gym bag and rummages around, taking out a small travel bag. He fusses with the opening of the bag and leaves it strategically open before entering the bathroom. Between the teeth of the zipper, I see it. The dildo is impossibly large, big around as a Coke bottle at the middle, and garishly colored in a pink flesh tone that is not quite human. He re-emerges.

"You want some of this?" He holds out a tiny mirror with two lines on it.

"What is it?"

"Just a little crissy. Get you in the mood." He laughs—a nervous, perfunctory burst.

"No thanks, you go ahead."

There are beads of sweat on his forehead. He smells funny. He lowers his head and I see the *V* of perspiration between his shoulder blades. He snorts, rubs his nostrils, licks his lips. His eyes water. I can hear his cotton mouth working.

"Do you actually use that big toy?" I ask.

"Yes, I love it."

"How?"

"What do you mean how? You just put it in."

"No, I mean, how can it fit?"

"It does, you just gotta practice and relax. I'll show you."

He peels off his pants and somehow gets them past his feet. He drops the aqua bikini brief. I have never before seen a Hitlerian pubic mustache in person, but I do not linger on it because something higher is unfolding. With his arms at his sides, he becomes lovely in his rounded stillness. My eyes survey him as he removes his socks. In the play of flesh across the sparrow-delicate bones of his rib cage, I see how god loves details. The bones of his pelvic crest push up and form a gently arching cup that holds his torso. His knees and rump are of a kind, dimpled and toothsome. He is like those Russian nesting dolls. A man with a lot of boy in him. A boy with a lot of girl in him.

By way of announcing the afternoon's agenda, he drops to his knees with his face in my pillow. His crack is shaved and lubed and I can see he's been fucked recently.

"Put it in, *gordito*."

"Really?"

"Yeah. Put it in."

I grab for the piece, obedient and awkward. My fingers don't quite meet around it so I hold it with two hands. I put it up to his hole. It doesn't look right: Tom trying to enter Jerry's little mouse door. Couldn't possibly work.

"Is something *wrong?*" he asks.

"Seems like this will hurt you."

"Put it in." he says. "It's fine, okay?"

"All right."

"And call me a bitch. You can call me a whore, okay? I like that."

"Okay," I say, pressing the toy to his hole and summoning my porno growl. "Yeeeah. You fuckin' bitch. You like it, don't you?"

"Yes, fuck me like a bitch."

"You're a little whore, aren't you?"

"Yes, put it in now. I want it now." I push and the great crowned head pops in. He backs up and several inches disappear. I'm in shock and try to pull it back out.

"Put it in, all the way in." I push forward, and feel the resistance increase.

"Yeah, all the way, *gordo*. Tell me what I am."

"You're a whore—and you like it. A dirty fucking whore." I begin pumping it in and out, and he gasps. I am enthralled and confused, wondering if he is totally in or completely out of his body. A line of blood trickles down the dildo.

"You're bleeding."

"It's okay, it does that, keep going."

I am frightened by his surrender. His open hunger. The bloody thread that creeps toward the base of the dildo, my tender hangnails, and my clean sheets.

"Hold on, okay? I'll get that blood."

I leave the toy halfway up his ass and run to the bathroom for a tissue.

"Here, lemme wipe that." I wipe and gingerly toss the tissue in the garbage. I run to the bathroom to wash. When I return, he speaks softly.

"You're really nice, *gordo*."

"Don't mention it."

"No, really. You are."

"You want me to take that dildo out?"

"Yeah, please," he says, suddenly self-conscious. I withdraw it slowly. He shudders. His hole is a raw crater. The elasticity is shot for now, and he doesn't quite close up. I can see the darkness inside, imagine the quiver of nerve endings. He fishes a towel out of his gym bag and swaddles the beast tightly, a filmy pink baby.

"You wanna fuck me, *gordo*?"

"I don't think it would be very satisfying after that monster. What could I do in there?"

"C'mon. Do it."

"I don't have condoms."

"Just do it anyways." He puts his face back in the pillow and spreads himself open. His thighs and glutes go taut. The muscles running up his back rear up, forming a sinewy valley around his spinal column. This guy parties like it's 1979. He is not afraid for himself. He is not afraid for me. My cock is throbbing. I curl my toes around the edge of the cliff.

"No," I exhale. "I don't think this is going to wo—"

"I can see you want to," he says, eyeing my crotch.

"Yeah, I do, but it's not going to happen today."

He pauses a beat and then replies, "I wanna suck your dick"

"Okay," I say. I pull it out and he begins sucking.

He yanks my pants down and I step out of them. He rubs my thighs and disengages. "Wow. You're not as fat as you look.

Lookit your legs, they're like rocks. You could be a Terminator if you ate more begetables and less carbohydras."

"Thanks."

"So do you wanna fuck me?"

"No. This is just fine."

"I want you to fuck me. I like toys. You got like a wine bottle or a baseball bat?"

"Baseball bat? Maybe. Lemme look."

I pad down the hallway. The apartment air is cold on my bare ass. I look in the storage pantry, remembering vaguely that my roommates had an aluminum bat on one of the shelves. As I climb on the stepladder I hear the key in the downstairs door. Fuck, my roommates Berto and Davey are home! I jump from the ladder and race through the kitchen, hoping to duck into my room before they get to the top of the landing and see me bare-assed. Behind me, I hear them lugging their groceries up the stairs. In the shotgun hallway, I pour on the speed, but halfway down the hall I step on a tiny area rug, and it goes out from under me. I fall movie style, in slow motion, feet in the air, arms flapping crazily, as if I could arrest the fall. My bare ass slaps against the hardwood, and the pain coruscates up my back. I roll over, and push through the pain in my tailbone, crawling the final yard to my door and kicking it closed with my foot as my roommates clear the landing.

I lie on the bedroom floor, curled up and rubbing my ass.

"Are you okay?"

"I fell. My back hurts."

"Do you need an ambulance?"

"No. I just need to lie down." I crawl to my bed, sucking air as my heart races. This is bad.

"Was that your family coming in?"

"No. Just friends. Roommates."

"Do you have sex with them?"

"No. They're just friends."

"Are they cute?"

"Not since I started living with them. Listen, this is not a good time to have this talk. Can you get your things together?"

"Okay. But if you won't have sex now, can you call me? We can have coffee or something. Maybe a movie." On a scrap of newspaper from his gym bag, he writes the name *Raul.*

"Call me, okay?"

"Okay. No problem."

I never again see him outside of my fantasies. For months to come, he will pop in to costar in my masturbatory epics. The scene is always a mirrored inversion of our true encounter. I am now the bossy one, the reckless one, the shameless one.

"What are you doing, gordo?" he asks me, and his face is all alarm and arousal.

"I'm fucking you the way you want it, bitch." He half protests but we both know he doesn't mean it. The fantasy climaxes with a skin-to-skin communion of animal simplicity. I perform magnificently, knowing that our sweat has transmuted the bed into a magic quadrant, where we finally grapple beyond disease and on the far side of dread. I almost don't want to release, and when I finally do, the smell of my cum is sharp and suffused with the grief of all the pleasures denied me. I lie there and pant as the cum cools on my belly. My breathing slows, and I fall asleep with my receding cock cradled in my hand.

RUDE AWAKENING

Doug Harrison

So I have a dick. A big dick, I think. And it squirts when I yank on it. So what? Don't all the guys do this? Big fuckin' deal. Well, not really—I haven't used it for fucking yet. Wonder when that will happen? Girls are confusing. I mean, you have to wine and dine them, pretend you don't crave their pussies and just want to know the "real" them, snuggle closer, warm them up, and slowly seduce them. It's their fault. They start this stupid game when they act like they don't want it. Yeah, sure.

Sam tells me his girlfriend gets wet fast. She locks her legs around his waist and rides him like he's a bucking bronco. He shoots fast. Then he has to finish her off with his finger, sometimes his fist, jabbing her gushing twat and twisting his hand like he was mixing some cruddy pie dough. I guess it's called fist fucking. Don't these prim and proper girls ever get enough? Like, how many times can they come? Well, look who's talking—sometimes I jerk off five times a day. I can't help myself—it feels so good. I wonder if I'd be more satisfied if I had a girl-friend?

Everybody seems to be getting laid except me. At least that's what they say. All these guys acting like studs. And they look like studs. Me, I'm the skinny one.

Joe, star quarterback, yelled at me the other day. In front of everybody, while I was rushing to my job at the shoe store. "Look at the pads in his jacket," he taunted. "No shoulders. I'll bet the sissy doesn't have any hair on his chest, either."

Yeah, he's right. No hair there, a little in my crotch and armpits. Everybody smirks when I undress for gym. Unless they look at my big dick. But I try to keep it covered. I wrap a towel around my thin, white hips when I rush to and from the shower, and face the wall while I quickly soap down. That's 'cause Dad says I shouldn't expose myself. And Mom says I shouldn't bend backward when I sway in time to the accordion music I'm play-ing at our high school talent reviews. Says I show my shape.

So, they're uptight. What else is new? She's Catholic and he's Congregational. Anyone who can find their way out of a paper bag knows I had to be raised Catholic. We're all dreadfully prim and proper in our little house in our small New England factory town.

And they never argue. Never even raise their voices. Pride themselves on "keeping things on an even keel." Sure wish I was being raised in an Italian family. Rather have too much emotion than none at all. No wonder they never discuss sex with me.

Thirteen years old, I'm already a freshman, and I wake up with a puddle in the bed. "Why the hell did I wet the bed?" I silently scream. "This never happened before—at least I don't remember it from when I was a baby. Why now?" I get up and try to clean the mess. It's sticky. Piss isn't sticky. I go back to sleep sobbing, "What's wrong with me?" I wake up and search the sheet; I find a Shmoo-shaped spot that's hard and crinkly. I hope Mom doesn't see it when she does the laundry. I think about it all day at school. At dinner that night Mom says Dad and her are taking me to the doctor the next day, right after school. I don't ask why.

So, I'm facing the doctor in his dimly lit office, tapping my fingers on the cracked Naugahyde chair, shuffling my feet, wondering why we aren't in the examination room. He seems far away; we're separated by a large desk covered with messy piles of papers, rumpled prescription pads, and a stethoscope coiled like two angry snakes. He leans back in his creaky swivel chair, folds his arms, thinks for a few seconds, and asks, "Doug, do you ever notice what's different about women?"

Well, right away I think about their big boobs, but I'm too embarrassed to say anything. I just sit there, head bowed, feeling as stupid as I probably look. So he explains to me about breasts, and vaginas, and penises, and how babies are made. I'm dumbfounded. I mean, like, I wasn't raised on a farm, and I don't have any rutting pets. And I can't imagine Dad and Mom doing *that*.

I shuffle out of the doctor's office, mind awhirl. Mom and Dad are waiting for me in the car. Nothing's said about my appointment. We go shopping. We're walking along the sidewalk, and I wait for a spot where there aren't many people, and I look over at Mom and ask, "Mom, how do the sperm know when to come out?" Her lips, lightly covered with crimson lipstick, make a real tight grin. She bites her tongue, but can't stop a smirk, which crescendos into laughter. She sashays to a parking meter, grabs it, and holds on as if buffeted by a hurricane. Her shoulders shake as she roars. Tears stream down her cheeks, leaving snail trails in her rouge. My father glowers at her, frozen and mute; he doesn't blink for a very long minute. Finally, his entire body shudders, like he's trying to breathe composure into our little scene, and he pleads in a whisper, "Please, dear, people are staring."

So, that's the beginning of my sex education. Not from my father. Not from my best buddy. But from a freakin' doctor! And I figure out how the sperm know when to come out. They have to be yanked out, cajoled by a clenched fist or a tight pussy. At least I hope they're tight, and not just smelly like I hear from Sam. Or maybe coaxed by a welcoming asshole. But that sounds yucky. I read about it in a sex book I thumbed through in the back of a bookstore. Well, I gotta admit, I went to that chapter first after glancing at the table of contents. Cripes, butt fucking is the one thing the doctor didn't mention.

It's my sophomore year. I'm tired of playing the accordion and I start organ lessons. My teacher, Robert, is the organist at the Congregational Church, and a Bach expert. He plays for me now and then, particularly when he's tightening up a difficult piece for performance. It's always just the two of us in the large church. His fingers glide effortlessly over the keys, and his hands jump among the four keyboards, sometimes crossing, and never missing a beat. He sits upright on the hard oak bench, but his upper body moves sensuously with the music. His black hair flaps to the beat if it's a vigorous piece. During a slow section, I can sense the cocoon of serenity surrounding the organ pit as the music expands from the distant ranks of pipes, filling the church and caressing the walls. Regardless of the pace or difficulty of the music, I'm amazed at how his feet slide over the curved pedal board, like a tap dancer's feet, seemingly unconnected to his body, but nonetheless contributing to the overall performance.

Is the music a reflection of his body, or his body a reflection of the music he's producing?

As the year progresses, Robert teaches me a lot about counterpoint and preludes and fugues. By the end of the summer, he also teaches me about having sex with a man. Scares the hell out of me. I guess I'm a prime piece of jailbait, but I don't turn him in. Not in our town—everyone would be embarrassed and mad and they'd all start talking about me, like I wanted it. Well, maybe I do.

Robert has spent the summer doing graduate work at some hoity-toity conservatory in Kentucky. I have my mother's blessing, and indeed, encouragement, to take an overnight train from our small town in Connecticut to Kentucky to help Robert pack his car and drive back with him. Little does she know. Or me, for that matter.

I get there. Robert tells me he had a roommate for the summer, some guy who moves out just before I arrive. But he leaves his bikini swimsuit drying on the bathtub. Kinda strange, I think. The suit's sheer and skimpy, almost transparent, and I sure wouldn't wear it to the swimming pool. But it turns me on, sorta. Well, to be honest, I'd like to try it on, but it looks too small.

Robert has one double bed. So where did this roommate guy sleep? *Uh-oh,* I think. It's night, and I'm real tired, and I undress and crawl in, bare-ass naked. I catch him sneaking glances at me, not at all relaxed like guys undressing in the gym. You know, no bantering. In fact, he doesn't say anything, just quickly strips with jerky motions, like a marionette with tangled strings. Where's Mr. Smooth Church Organist now?

Partway through his strip un-tease, he turns off the light. But I have time to notice that his thin, almost hairless torso echoes his bony fingers, and his chest, like his angular face, is pockmarked.

He moves too quickly for me to see his crotch. I turn on my side, facing away from him. I try to fall asleep, but my hands are clammy, and I keep wiggling back and forth, trying to get closer to the edge of the bed without falling off. Robert slowly follows me, like a panther tracking a helpless deer trapped near the end of some dark canyon. He snuggles up against me, reaches over my shoulder, and rubs my chest. It feels good, even though his fingers tremble a little. I swallow hard so he can't hear me beginning to moan with pleasure. *It's just a massage,* I think. *But we're in bed,* a little voice in my head adds. I'm scared, but I sorta want it, whatever it is gonna be.

Robert reaches for my crotch, and there it is—my big boner. I can't help it; it won't go away. "Ah," he sighs. He strokes my shaft, more than a handful, and squeezes it, tight, loose, tight, loose, like pushing toothpaste along a half-empty tube. I feel his hard-on sliding between my legs. The odor of spit hangs in the air. He rubs the palm of his hand over the end of my dick; it's almost too intense despite all the juice I'm leaking. I shudder, I let myself groan, my hips jerk, and I come right away. I mean, really come, like I'm dizzy. Then Robert squirts all over my butt. He must've been fucking me between my legs, but I didn't even notice. Of course it's sticky, but he doesn't clean it up. Just falls asleep and starts snoring.

I'm trembling. Have I lost my virginity? Does this count? God, I have to go to confession in two weeks. I know Father Shaw will recognize my voice from the other side of the confessional screen. "Bless me, Father, for I have sinned. My last confession was one month ago. I missed mass once, I sassed my mother three times, I played with myself lots, and I had sex with a man." What's he gonna think? He's one of the local judges in the statewide "Let Freedom Ring" essay contest I entered. Shit! I wish I'd stayed home. I'm tossing and turning, motor-mind in full gear, but I finally tumble into an exhausted sleep.

In the morning Robert asks me what I want for breakfast, like nothing happened. I can't look him in the eye. If we were back home, I could hide.

I might as well be his prisoner for the next three days and two nights as we drive eight hundred miles north. I survive, though. We trade off driving his big Pontiac. I look straight ahead a lot, and don't say much. Neither does he.

We have sex one more time in some motel. It's easier because Robert does exactly the same thing. But dammit, he acts like he's entitled—I mean, he never discusses his intentions. And I still don't discuss how I feel; I'm too shy and scared to talk about sex. I don't know what to say anyway. But he's the grown-up; shouldn't he say something, anything?

Robert and I get it on a few more times after we're back. The last time, we do it in his large house, while his mother's in the other wing. God, I'm anxious. Will she interrupt us? Or, could be, she knows what's going on. I know I'm cute, so maybe she's figured out why I'm the only one Robert wants to listen to records with. It doesn't matter. I'm having enough trouble with my own identity to worry about his. My Catholic guilt churns in me while we're doing it. And afterward too. I don't think Robert ever notices my nervousness, or cares, because he doesn't look me in the eye. And his hands still tremble when he reaches for me, so I sure do look at him, straight on. Makes me feel a little better, like I'm learning, even if he isn't.

Gosh, all this is too confusing. I like having sex with another person. And I know Robert and me can't be open. But I want Robert to show he cares about me. I guess I feel like a girl must feel. Maybe this wining and dining stuff isn't a bad idea after all.

THE SECOND DATE

Jonathan Asche

When Harris suggested going for a walk in the park after dinner I thought he was being romantic. I didn't think he meant *this* park.

I knew it well, this scraggly patch of land separating a residential neighborhood from a dilapidated business district, occupied by pot-smoking teens during the day, men on the prowl at night. Already, in the early evening, I could see the men gathering. Some sat in their cars, waiting to see what happened by, while others wandered the grounds, trolling. Across the park, near the restrooms, a man in white shorts did a slow stroll within a circle of light cast from a lamppost in front of the squat cinder-block building. Another man, in blue jeans and a black T-shirt, leaned against the building, one foot hitched up against the wall, smoking a cigarette, ignoring the guy in white shorts and looking right at us.

I fought back the memory: me on the floor in a toilet stall, the coppery flavor of a stranger's cum in my mouth, my own jizz soaking my T-shirt and matted in my pubic hair. When I opened my eyes—

"You look lost in thought," Harris said.

My chest felt as if it were in a vise. Did he *know* about my past? "It's this park. It's a little, um, creepy."

"*Cruisy* would be a better description."

Could've told you that when you suggested coming here, I thought.

We first met at the grocery store, of all places. He caught my attention in produce. I saw him over by the prepackaged salads: around my age; dark hair buzzed down close to his scalp; cutting a nice figure, with an ass practically gift-wrapped in blue jeans. Our paths crossed again in dairy, and I got a closer view. I checked him out from the crotch up. By the time I completed my slow pan upward and reached his face he was smiling at me. I returned an embarrassed smile before hurrying past him.

He caught up with me in frozen foods, saying he thought he recognized me from somewhere. I said, "Probably from produce," and he laughed. Awkward small talk—and for me *all* small talk is awkward—followed, ending with him asking me out.

The first date—your standard dinner-and-a-movie package—went well. I guess. Well enough for Harris to ask me out again, even though we didn't have sex.

That's right. No sex on the first date. My therapist's idea, her thinking being that by abstaining I could concentrate on relating to Harris as a person, opening the door to greater intimacy, blah, blah, blah. Easy for her to say; I wanted to blow him in the grocery store parking lot the night we met. You can take the queen out of the tearoom...

But when Harris kissed me goodnight, I said: "I don't have

sex on the first date." I even sounded halfway convincing. Still, if he pressed I would've reneged on my vow in a heartbeat.

"There's always the second date," he said, his voice a velvety purr, making my cock twitch. I was jacking off about five minutes after Harris left me at my apartment.

Now, in the park, he said, "I have an idea," winking and grabbing my hand.

We were heading to the restrooms. "What did you have in mind?" I was trying to choke back my rising panic.

Harris disengaged his hand from mine, moving it to the small of my back. He leaned in and said, "Thought we could have some fun with these guys."

The man in the white shorts ducked away into the shadows, behind a tree, as we neared the restrooms. The smoker remained at his spot against the buildings wall, staring at us brazenly. Thirty-ish, about average height, an okay body: attractive enough that he could go to any one of the city's gay bars and get a man and not have to skulk about a public park on a Friday night. He shot me a lecherous grin and slid a hand down to the mound in his crotch and squeezed it lewdly.

Like he was on to me.

I looked away, my stomach tightening. Harris's mischievous smile had hardened into something more sinister as he pulled me forward to the battered men's room door.

My heart was in my throat by the time we stepped into the restroom's dim interior. Only one of the light fixture's three fluorescent rods was functioning; one was dead and another was dying, flickering intermittently like a slow-motion strobe. The walls were covered in cracked, mud-colored tile, beige enamel and obscene graffiti. The humid air smelled of mildew and stale piss.

Harris pushed me up against the wall opposite the sinks. He kissed me so hard I thought he might draw blood. My hands clamped onto his ass, my fingers tingling in anticipation of feeling the flesh beneath his pants.

A cough startled us. At the end of the room, standing against the wall just outside the last toilet stall, a man watched us. He was older than either of us, at least forty, his face hidden behind a full beard and a blue T-shirt hugging his barrel chest. Even in the weak light, the outline of his stiff cock in his jeans was plain, and he fondled it incessantly.

"Maybe we should go someplace else," I pleaded, my voice quavering.

Harris's hand went to my crotch. "Feels like you want to stay."

Suddenly, he grabbed my arm and pulled and we were on the move again, me stumbling behind him, heading toward the man standing at the end of the restroom. He greeted us with an impassive stare, waiting to see, as was I, what Harris had in mind.

"Show us your cock," Harris said in a low voice.

The man's eyes went from Harris to me. "Okay," he nodded. "Your boyfriend can do the honors."

"I think we should—"

But Harris pushed me forward. "You heard the man. Take his cock out of his pants."

With shaky fingers I unfastened the man's pants, trying not to look at him as I did so. He wasn't wearing any underwear. His rigid cock sprang forward the moment I opened his fly. Its girth was more impressive than its length; it was topped with a snub-nosed head. I gave it only the briefest glance, embarrassed to admire it too blatantly in front of Harris.

"Go ahead and touch it." The man's voice was like smoke.

"He'll do better than that," Harris said conspiratorially, pushing open the stall door. "C'mon, baby. Get in there, like when we first met."

Not in the grocery store. Two months ago:

I was there, on the floor in a toilet stall, a stranger's cum covering my face, my own jizz soaking my T-shirt and matted in my pubic hair. When I opened my eyes I discovered I wasn't alone. The door to the stall was open. Someone was standing there, watching me. I saw brown shoes, khaki pants, and a nice bulge in the crotch. By the time my eyes reached the intruder's face, he'd turned to flee. All I got was an intriguing glimpse, and he was gone. And then I was alone.

"It was you." My voice was dry and hoarse.

I was propelled forward into the stall. On my left, framed by scrawled messages promising good times and nine-inch dicks, a glory hole had been crudely cut into the plywood of the dividing wall. I spun around to face Harris, and saw him directing the stranger to the neighboring stall. My eyes were more questioning than angry, and when Harris saw me, he answered with an encouraging smile.

I knelt on the gritty cement floor. Seconds later, the stranger's cock appeared through the glory hole. Harris stood at the stall's entrance, holding the door open, his smile gone now. He nodded, and I turned my attention to the cock poking into my stall, leaning forward and closing my mouth around it. A deep sigh sounded from the other side of the wall as I took the dick deep into my throat, my lips traveling down the thick shaft.

The air was filled with heavy breathing, sudden gasps, constant wet slurping—me sucking a stranger's cock. The stall divider shook as the man on the other side thrust his bulk forward. I forgot about renouncing my past and I forgot about Harris watching me. I sucked the mystery man's cock harder, eager for its creamy reward. My dick ached, and I massaged it through my pants. I didn't unzip yet, not trusting myself to control my strokes.

The squeak of the door opening sent a chill through me—
what if it's the cops?—but my fear was quickly eased by the
stranger's loud grunts. "Oh, fuck yeah!" he groaned between
strangled breaths.

His cock erupted in my mouth. I pulled away, letting his load
splash onto my face. I rubbed the throbbing head against my
smooth cheek. Grabbing the shaft, I squeezed the last drop of
splooge onto my tongue.

The stranger's cock retreated through the hole. Grunts, sighs,
zipping, the shuffling of feet, and he was gone.

Did Harris have his cock out now? I wondered. Was he jacking off? Did he want me to suck *his* cock? I was about to turn
and see, but then another anonymous dick was offered to me,
bigger than the last: at least eight inches, only partially erect.
This cock also had the distinction of being uncut, its head still
tucked within its sleeve of pink flesh.

Harris would have to wait his turn.

Gripping the semihard rod, I gently chewed the tip, the salty
taste of precum leaking out from the wrinkled folds of foreskin.
Slowly, I pulled back the prick's collar, revealing a fat, purplish
head. My tongue prodded the fleshy folds, allowing the foreskin
to roll back up, trapping my tongue against the head. I wiggled
my tongue back and forth, enjoying the extra skin I had to play
with. The uncut cock's owner trembled, making the wall between us shake.

The cock stiffened in my mouth, taking my own arousal to
an excruciating level. My dick *hurt*, I was so horny. I'd be freeing it soon, but not yet. It was a challenge I often made myself
endure back when: how many cocks could I suck before I gave
in to the urge to get myself off. To date, I'd managed four before
caving. My self-made dare was partly for the agonizing thrill it
gave me, my cock aching in my pants, neglected. But on a more

practical level, I delayed touching myself because I knew once I came the spell would be broken.

A shadow fell over me as someone joined me in the stall. I turned to my left, expecting to see Harris but finding another stranger instead. He was young—early-twenties, I guessed—with a slender frame. A curtain of long brown hair fell forward as he looked at me, shadowing his face. Tight, faded blue jeans hugged his narrow hips, the worn denim stretching over a pronounced bulge. Wordlessly, the young man unfastened his pants quickly and presented me with his beautiful cock. It was a decent length, well formed and, like most dicks I saw, cut.

But I made this new guy wait, turning back to the uncut member poking through the hole, now fully hard and throbbing, the foreskin stretched back to reveal the purplish head. I sucked on it a minute, reminding the man I hadn't forgotten him, simultaneously reaching for the young guy standing next to me, stroking his cock while I swallowed another.

The young man stepped closer, and my mouth jumped from the uncut guy to this less anonymous cock. The young guy's dick disappeared deep into my gullet. I could feel him shudder, and he let out an involuntary "Oh!" He didn't trim his pubes—my nose sank into a cushion of coarse, curly hairs as I deep-throated him.

Abruptly, I returned to the uncut cock, sucking it in swift, long gulps. The stranger hissed and there was a hard *thunk* as he rammed his hips forward against the plywood wall. Next came the flood of semen, washing over my tongue. I pulled my head back and held the cockhead against my lips, letting its spurts land on my face, the jism slowly sliding down either side of my mouth.

I gave the uncut cock's sticky head a kiss before it retreated. Through the hole I saw a glimpse of white fabric and wondered if I'd just sucked off the guy in white shorts Harris and I had seen outside earlier.

Back to the young guy. His cock was drooling now, a long gossamer string of precum suspended from its head. Leaning forward, I stretched my tongue to catch the salty juices oozing from his dick. He pressed the engorged crown onto my tongue, squeezing out another trickle of precum. My lips came down, tightening around the shaft, trapping the young stranger's cock inside my mouth.

As I sucked him, I tugged at the front of his pants, pulling them down to reveal his balls. His ball sac was drawn up tight, the wiry hairs covering the scrotum standing on end, as if filled with static electricity. I nuzzled the fuzzy nut sac with my chin as I nibbled at the base of his cock. My tongue prodded the cum-engorged orbs, making the young stranger hiss and grab a fistful of my hair.

I returned my mouth to his dick, relishing the feel of it sliding against my tongue and pushing against the walls of my throat. I swallowed every inch of him, and I wanted more.

The young man withdrew, suddenly. He started to stroke himself, his cock lubricated with my spit and his own juices.

A husky voice interrupted. "Cum on his face."

My young stranger was startled at the sound of Harris's voice, his hand flying away from his dick as if it were scalding hot. Harris's sudden appearance startled me, too; in my lusty delirium I'd nearly forgotten he was there at all. Harris nodded, wordlessly indicating the young man should continue. The expression on his face was somewhere between awe and catatonia. His gaze shifted from me to the stranger's cock, now aimed at my face and ready to shoot.

I closed my eyes and waited, listening to the wet, flabby sound of the young man pulling on his cock at a feverish pace. Then:

a groan exploded from the young man's mouth, milliseconds before his load exploded from his cock. Warm, heavy droplets splashed down on my forehead, hit my nose, and singed the tip of my tongue. "Oh, yeah," whispered Harris. I opened my eyes then, catching the young stranger in the final spasms of his orgasm—his mouth slack, his body trembling, his cock oozing. Harris had his hands on the young man's shoulders, massaging them as he said something into his ear. The stranger pushed his dick downward, forcing his hard-on to meet my tongue. Making contact, he wiped the last thick drop of splooge onto my greedy taste buds.

A moment later, my young friend was stuffing his cock back in his pants, careful not to look at me, or in Harris's direction, and then scurrying out of the stall like he'd just stolen something.

It was just Harris and me now. I watched intently as he undid his pants, my eyes glued to the swell pushing against the fabric. His pants unbuttoned and unzipped, he exposed himself with one quick tug. His cock was so rigid it fell forward only slightly, parallel with his flat stomach. Finally seeing it—its dark tan shaft, its almost pointy head, the precum beading on the tip— made my lips tremble. Of all the cocks I'd seen, tonight and on every night before tonight, this was the one I wanted the most.

I started to reach for Harris's cock, eager to taste it, but he shoved me away, making me fall onto my ass. He was smiling the same conspiratorial smile he wore when he first pushed me into the stall. Bending down, he reached for me, hooking a hand around my biceps and hauling me to my feet in the same forceful manner he'd pushed me away.

Harris studied my face, and raised a hand to brush away a lock of sweaty hair that fell across my forehead. After this pretense of tenderness, he seized me violently, shoving me to the back wall, our bodies wedged between the stall's dividing wall and the toilet. He forced his tongue into my mouth, his hands pulling on my belt, his cock pressing against my leg.

I responded with equal vigor, my tongue twisting around his while my hands groped wildly, pulling at his shirt, grabbing for his dick. Harris lost patience fumbling with my pants and jerked them open, the top button popping off and clattering onto the floor. He kissed and licked my face, lapping up the sticky souvenirs left by the anonymous cocks I'd sucked, his mouth returning to mine to share the taste. My pants were pulled down with one decisive yank, my tortured dick freed.

Harris forced three fingers into my mouth, and I sucked them the way I wanted to suck his cock. When he withdrew his fingers, they were dripping with my saliva. Thus lubricated, Harris's fingers slid in between my buttcheeks.

"I'm gonna fuck you so hard," he snarled, pushing his fingertips past my asslips, making me writhe.

Harris held his other hand below my lips and commanded me to spit into his palm. Just as I'd lubricated his fingers for fingering my hole, I was to provide lubrication for his cock. He handled himself almost delicately as he smeared the handful of my viscous saliva around his pulsating rod while his other hand continued to play with my asshole.

Once he'd lubricated his cock, his hand went to his back pocket, returning with a rubber. My breathing was hard and ragged as I watched him tear open the condom packet with his teeth, pull out the rubber and unroll it over his wet cock, impressed he could do it with only one hand. He pulled his fingers out of my hole and brought that hand back to my face, giving me a whiff of my own musk.

"Spit," he said.

I hocked a big gob into his smelly palm, expecting this to

be the lube for his sheathed cock. Instead, his hand grasped my aching pole. My body twisted and jerked like I'd been hit with a stun gun.

"I'm so close…," I said through clenched teeth. "You keep that up I'm gonna cum."

"That's the idea."

A burst of pleasure erupted and shot out my cock. For a split second I saw my formidable load spurt, caught by Harris's other hand. Then I closed my eyes, my body weakening and my head growing light.

When I opened my eyes, Harris was rubbing his hard-on, coating the condom with my hot jism.

"Turn around," he ordered.

I faced the back wall and Harris clamped a hand around my neck, pushing me forward, forcing me to bend down. I braced myself against the tile.

He entered me with surprising care, easing his dick into my chute one deliberate inch at a time. Still, the pain was unavoidable, each advance of his cock searing my sphincter as it was stretched wider and wider. I bit the inside of my mouth, keeping my discomfort to myself. I knew pleasure would soon follow.

We stopped moving: Harris was all the way inside me, his silky pubic hair tickling the crack of my ass. The pain of his entry had waned, overtaken by the pleasurable tension of his cock buried in me.

We started moving: first Harris, thrusting his hips forward in steady strokes; and then me, pushing backward to meet him. We were quiet at first, the only sound that of his sinewy thighs hitting my ass and the squish of his cock sliding in and out of my hole, lubricated by my juice. But as Harris began to pick up the pace, so, too, did our noise level increase: hard breathing, grunts, gasps, and groans. Anyone walking by the restrooms could've heard us, but at that moment I didn't care.

Harris called me a *filthy slut* and *cum whore*—names I'd called myself all the way into therapy, but now they went right to my cock, bringing it back to life after its brief respite. He rammed me viciously, his body crouched over mine, each thrust pushing my face against the stall's grimy wall. One hand gripped my waist, the other pulled on my collar, ripping the fabric. His breathing raged loud in my ear.

Harris froze, suddenly, emitting a sound like he'd been punched in the gut.

"Oh, *yessss*," I hissed as he came, feeling his cock pulse against my asslips as it pumped out its load.

We sank to the floor, his dick still deep in my chute. We lay together on the stall's dirty floor, Harris nibbling at the nape of my neck, playing with my cock—fully hard again, throbbing to his touch—and me, my heart racing, feeling the rise and fall of his chest pressed against my sweaty back as he struggled to catch his breath. I smiled, thinking how my therapist was right after all: it was worth the wait.

Brian's pouring pancake batter onto the skillet. I take orange juice from the fridge and fill the six small glasses on the table. "Why six?" I ask.

"We'll have a guest this morning," Brian says. "Someone who may be joining us."

I look down at my pajamas, chalk-blue hospital scrubs. A white robe, threadbare as an old washcloth. "I should have showered and dressed before breakfast."

"Nah, don't worry." Brian is still smiling. "That's 'past life' thinking, Paul. You look fine."

I feel better, at least until Davy and Aaron and Todd appear. Davy and Aaron have showered and dressed in the preferred manner, in oversized sweatshirts and sweatpants. Todd's still in his pajamas, but they look like they've been ironed, for Christ's sake. And his slippers are stylish and gleaming, not mangy looking. I'm grateful, after we've said our good mornings, to take a seat and hide my hairy white ankles from view.

"We *were* going to have a guest this morning," Brian says, carrying a platter of pancakes to the table. "But he's late. You know what that means, he might not show. So I'm not holding up breakfast."

Mixed reactions around the table. Aaron and Todd look slightly disappointed, while Davy, who's the nervous type, looks relieved. Me, I'm staring at my silverware.

"Anybody have a dream last night?" Brian asks, as he usually does.

My silverware-staring has yielded strange fruit. "Wait," I cry. "Wait, wait, wait." I tug on Davy's sleeve.

"What is it?" he asks.

The small hairs on the back of my neck are rising. "Does my fork match my spoon match my knife?"

"What?"

"My fork match my spoon match my—"

"Take it easy, Paul."

Take it easy? Doesn't anybody understand why I'm upset? My *knife*, my *fork*, my *spoon*—in a house where no two plates or glasses match, where every freaking cup and saucer came from a different garage sale, it's *impossible* that two pieces of silverware would match, let alone a spoon *and* a fork *and* a knife....

"I see what he means," Brian says. "It's true, they all have the same pattern. What are the odds?"

Now they're all peering at my silverware. "Huh," Aaron says.

Brian laughs. "Well, don't worry, Paul. Just because your tableware matches doesn't mean you're a fag."

Har har har.

"Yeah," Todd says, "it doesn't mean you don't like pussy."

This kind of talk is allowed, to an extent. Not that we're

intended to be sexist pigs in training; it's just that...well, we're *guys*, that's all, and that's what guys are like. Todd ought to know—Todd of the tall slender frame and sarcastic voice, Todd whose skin holds a deep boyish tan even in the dead of winter. *It's precisely the nape of his neck that I love to suck and lick and nibble at. There's nothing better in the world—unless it's the smooth salty edge of his shoulder blade or the funky shallows of his navel.*

Surprisingly strong, he slings me up against the headboard, excited to see my shoulders thump wood. If I look scared, so much the better. "Go ahead," I tell him, raising my knees. "Fuck me, hurt me, leave a mark that'll never go away." First he lowers his face toward mine, having something to prove with his tongue, turning my mouth inside out from bicuspid to tonsil. When I can't stand waiting any longer I beg shamelessly. "Fuck me, you know you want to, your balls are gonna burst, give it to me...!" When he's good and ready, he does.

"Hey, Paul?" Aaron asks, barely concealing his mirth. "Do your sheets match, too?"

You ought to know, I nearly tell him. Oh, Aaron! How quickly our physical relationship evolves from after-dinner hand jobs to free-for-alls. Here you come, stocky and bristly, musky in your hairy crevices, lumbering on hands and knees across my twisted bedclothes like an animal too big to be cute, that monster cock swinging halfway down your thigh. Is this part of the appeal of being gay—the scary-funhouse side of it, when some brute rolls toward you with a boner that could cleave you in two? "Please don't hurt me, please." Yet it's a cinch to roll you over on your back—heavier men can be light on their knees—and snap goes the strip of leather around your scrotum, stretching your balls; snap goes the cock ring, preparing your tool for worship. Erect and glistening, it shivers against the tip of

my tongue, which can tease hard cock like nothing else on earth.
I bring you to the brink, then switch to your heavy balls, jug-
gling them with my tongue. Then back to your dick, then your
balls, dick, balls, dick, and I haven't even started on your asshole
yet. By the time I do you're grinding your buttcheeks against
my face, whimpering like a cub. When you can't take any more
you grab me by the hair, caveman style, and pull me toward the
head of the bed. Your cock looms like one of those alien space-
ships that fill half the movie screen. You'll use my mouth like a
cunt, then flip me over and ream my asshole till I'm almost dead.
Whatever's left of me can be used to scrub our juices from the
sheets. I'll be an old cum rag, crumpled and crusty, abandoned
at the side of the bed.

The doorbell rings at last. Brian leaves to answer it, and in
a moment—has it only been a moment?—he returns with our
guest in tow, a slim young man in his twenties with a mustache
and dark, heavy eyebrows that give him a skeptical look. He
seems nervous, like me, and I'm glad his seat is down at the end
of the table.

"Everybody, this is Kent," Brian says. "Kent, meet David,
Aaron, Todd, and Paul."

Kent nods, a lock of dark brown hair falling across his forehead. He smoothes it back—a delicate gesture, tellingly so. He
sits down and, with some effort, moves his heavy captain's chair
closer to the table.

"This is a typical Sunday morning," Brian says, returning to
the griddle. "Up at nine, something special for breakfast—and
these pancakes *are* special, if I do say so myself. Uh, we don't
have religious services here, I think I told you that."

"Yeah, I don't care about that," Kent says. He glances in dismay at the two pancakes Brian's sliding onto his plate. "I forgot
to tell you, I already ate breakfast."

Brian laughs. "It's all right, Kent, we don't put anything in the food. Have some coffee, anyway." He fills Kent's cup from the carafe and takes his seat at the head of the table. "And think about this." He leans forward, steepling his fingertips, making eye contact. "Everything that worries you about your life…all the complications, the pain, the guilt…all of it gone. Does that sound like a better world?" He pauses for a beat. "You bet it does."

Brian's a force to be reckoned with, all right. His blue eyes, startling in their intensity, make up for the rest of his face, the blunt nose and the weak chin that always bears a few scrapes, as if he uses a razor made for larger, more challenging chins. No wonder Kent is squinting at him in deep concentration. Or maybe his contacts are bothering him.

"Now," Brian says, "I'm not telling you it's easy to change, but in the right environment it can be done. And we have that right here at East Oak House."

Kent's eyes, breaking loose from Brian's, light upon his fork, his napkin, the tub of low-fat margarine, their restlessness a symptom of the urge to change. It's almost too private a thing to witness, and I look down into my lap.

Brian asks Kent if he wants to take a tour of the place, and as Kent leaves his chair I get a good look at him again. His button-down shirt is open at the neck, revealing a nice serving of chest hair. His jeans define the trunk of his body a bit too well. A ring of keys hangs from his right-side belt loop. In the old days that would have meant he liked to get fucked—do key codes still apply?

"Be right back," Brian says, and they disappear up the back stairs, around the corner from the kitchen. I'm ready to take my coffee into the den, the only room where smoking is allowed, but for the moment it's good to sit and bask in my relief that our encounter with the stranger is over.

Todd gives a nervous cough. "He seems nice enough," he says, his voice unintentionally dripping with sarcasm.

"He didn't seem as nervous as I was," Davy says.

Like you *are*, I'm thinking, watching his orange juice tremble as he raises it to his lips. Just yesterday afternoon, as I'm dozing in the lumpy wing chair in the living room—unobtrusively, I hope, since there was a group session going on—a sound, unvarying like the droning of a jet overhead, originates nearby. I cuff my ear like a dog with a sudden itch, but the sound remains.

Focus, Paul. Get with the program, as Brian would say, *before it's too late.*

Okay, the sound can charitably be called a human voice: Davy's recounting, for the tenth or maybe the hundredth time, the source of his shame. Logy as I am, I recognize where he is in the story immediately: *He touched me.*

"He touched me," Davy says, choking back a sob.

He being the evil uncle, *me* being Davy at the tender age of thirteen. And now we're at the part where Brian says, *Yes, David, go on.*

"Yes, David, go on," Brian says.

"He *touched* me," Davy says, "and...oh, God...it felt so *exciting....*"

The abuse lasts through Davy's junior year in high school, ending with the uncle's mysterious disappearance. By then the damage has been done. Davy's giving blow jobs behind the school stadium every afternoon between three and four. He explains his late arrival home every day by saying he's joined Glee Club. The jocks who use his mouth know when they've got a good thing; they're not about to squeal.

"And how did it feel, David," Brian asks, "when they had all gone, and you were left alone there, behind the stadium?"

Wiping your chin. No, Paul, stop it.

Davy's beyond speaking now, tears are rolling. *Clothed, his slight frame promises little; but what a torso he's got—not bulky but chiseled; his pale, pale abs like dinner rolls waiting to be browned. They're as sensitive to touch as they are beautiful to look at, and more than once I've pinned him down and dug my fingers in, tickling him till he wet the bed.*

Now I have a new strategy: to become the best uncle he's ever had. I'll be the pat on his back, the cup of hot chocolate, the brisk walk through fallen leaves. I'll be the lap that's always open, the helpful hand on his zipper, and the dick that just...won't...stop.

Look at me now, shaking the way Davy does. I've had too much coffee this morning, with too much sugar. Which doesn't stop me from helping myself to another cup, and two more heaping teaspoons.

"Seems like Dwight's been gone a long time," Aaron says.

"I miss Dwight," Todd says. "I mean, as a friend."

I miss Dwight too. He came here not long before I did, and already he's gone. Well, recovery is different for everyone, as Brian would say. In group Dwight had a nice self-deprecating sense of humor. He was so fair his hair was almost white. *His chest hair too, thick and lickable. Nipples so sensitive that breathing on them made him sigh. When his dick got hard it was the darkest part of him. He had a funny dickhead, like a knob of putty stuck off-center. I liked to ride it while he bucked like a bronco. "Fuck me, stud. Fuck me till dawn and I'll slap your tits, just the way you like it."*

I got Dwight with one daring move. I don't know where I got the balls. It was one morning when I was passing him in the hall. He's traipsing toward the downstairs bathroom with a towel around his waist. I've never seen a man like him before: so pale,

yet so hairy. His nipples peek out through cotton-candy nests.
Oh, they ache to be touched, and my fingertips ache for them.

Who's to say, really, what's a friendly gesture between men?
I've seen enough grabassing in "straight" locker rooms to know
what a fuzzy line there can be between improper and acceptable
touch…. And so I talk myself, during this few seconds' walk
down the hallway, into reaching out with my right hand and
tweaking Dwight's left nipple as he passes. Without stopping he
reaches to slap my hand, letting loose a good-natured chuckle as
he misses it. I don't stop, either, but look back over my shoulder
to see him glancing at me. As I keep looking he swings around
on his large bare feet and walks back a few steps, facing me
full on as his towel suddenly slips from where his left hand was
grasping it—slips all the way to the floor. How embarrassing!
Yet there's a pause—a significant pause—before he stoops to
grab the towel. I see how the white fur continues down his belly
to his groin, see the pink tip of his dick, which swings in the lazy
arc peculiar to dicks in the process of lengthening, thickening….
As Dwight tucks his towel in place again, I catch his eye. Yes,
there's something there, in the half curve of his smile.

Dwight teaches me so much about tits: working them with
slick fingertips, I can master his entire body, cause different
parts to twitch uncontrollably—buttocks, thighs, feet. And he
never fails to look at me with gratitude that I so quickly found
his weakness, his obsession, his reason for living.

But what was his reason for leaving? Of course there's only
one reason to have: he had recovered. On the morning he told
us, he made a speech about life and change, presenting his case
with sincerity and skill. But why he chose that exact time to
go…racking my brain gives me no answers, and if I were really
honest I wouldn't need one. Instead I'd admit the truth: he left
because he didn't need us anymore.

Davy gets seconds on orange juice. I warm up my coffee again. By the time we've sat down Brian and Kent return, single file, Kent ducking into the kitchen as Brian, behind him, asks, "Well, what do you think?"

"It's pretty nice," Kent says.

So young. He looks young enough to be in high school, and he speaks—shades of Todd!—like a kid talking to a teacher, saying the right words but really thinking *You're full of shit*. Oh, he likes to get fucked, all right: it's as clear as the smile beneath his untrimmed mustache. How about that mustache? Why doesn't he keep it straight-edged? He must think that ragged fringe curling against his lip looks sexy, and damned if it doesn't. I know you, Kent: you're a little sex machine, working your sphincter around a lubricated shaft like you were born to do it; in mouth or ass you can take two cocks at once, sucking them up like a Dirt Devil.

I wonder what Brian has seen. Does he feel that Kent is a good candidate? Hard to tell from his expression. "Well," he says, sticking to the script, "I'm going to leave you all for a bit, so you guys can, you know, talk amongst yourselves." He takes his coat from the rack and edges through the kitchen door— making a show of leaving the house so that Kent won't think he's hiding somewhere, listening.

Taking his seat at the table again, Kent looks at each of us in turn, seeking eye contact. "So you guys aren't…?"

We sit perfectly still, as if we've put our heads together and decided to let composure speak for itself. Even Davy manages not to fidget.

"Nobody likes to suck dick? You don't even like to look at pictures of naked guys?"

Continued composure. Unruffled feathers.

"Jesus," Kent says, "don't you guys even *beat off?*"

My composure breaks, in the form of a short, sharp laugh that sounds and feels more like a sneeze.

Davy speaks up clearly and calmly. "You might not believe it now," he says, "but it's possible to lead a life where you're not obsessed with sex all the time. It's possible."

Kent sticks his tongue in his cheek, rolls it around as if tasting something new.

Sunday breakfast is followed by free time—a reminder that we're "free" from the burdens of churchgoing and other religious rot. I head for the den, where I can stare at the book-lined walls and smoke one cigarette after another. The only other smoker here is Brian, who keeps trying to quit. He'll duck into the room, light up and start pacing, biting drags off his fag, crushing it out when it's half gone. I said to him once, "If you're going to smoke, you might as well enjoy it," then wished I hadn't, for he looked even more ashamed. If you can forsake blow jobs, doesn't it follow that you should be able to stop sucking on Marlboros?

I don't see Brian during this Sunday morning smoke because he's left to get supplies; Kent has already decided he'll be moving in tonight. So I sit and smoke and listen to the winter complaints of the house and Davy's noodling on the living room piano. Todd and Aaron are probably upstairs, reading or perhaps writing letters with the standard apologies: *Sorry you can't visit me here, sorry we can't talk on the phone, sorry I can't even give you the address. Sorry, sorry, sorry. Those are the rules....*

The slamming of the kitchen door wakes me. Christ, have I been dozing with a lit cigarette in my hand? I check my hand, my lap, the chair, the floor, the ashtray. Nothing burning. The kitchen noise means that Brian is back from his shopping; I couldn't have slept very long. Long enough, though, for a thousand tiny dreams, and I close my eyes to try to recapture some.

The doorknob rattles. When the door swings open I expect to see Brian, hunchbacked with guilt, fitting a cigarette to his lips. Instead I see a cigarette, but the man it's attached to is Kent. He's startled to see me, his eyebrows go up—or rather eyebrow, for it's more like a single line hooding both eyes.

"Sorry," he says.

It takes me a moment to respond. "That's all right," is what finally comes out, though the pause before it makes it sound like a lie. "I just came in," I explain, "to look for a book." Yet it must be obvious, from the pack of cigs beside me and the butts in the ashtray, that I came here to smoke and smoke and smoke. There is a book, though, on my lap—*The Canterbury Tales*.

No jazz musician ever handled his mouthpiece the way Kent handles a cigarette. He takes a drag, rolls the taste around, lets it go in a thin line like escaping steam. He takes another drag, tilts his head back and, blinking rapidly, exhales through his nose. Finally he looks at me again, takes a step in my direction. My back stiffens against the chair—*What am I afraid of?*—and I think I might actually cry out till I see he's only heading for the ashtray by my right elbow.

"Sorry to interrupt you," he says, mixing his ash with mine.

"Oh, no, not at all. I was just..." What? Haven't I already told him I was looking for a book? I open *The Canterbury Tales* to the famous illustration of the Pardoner. This character's corrupt as hell: by Chaucer's time the selling of pardons had become a stinking rotten business. A critic named Kittredge even called the Pardoner "the one lost soul among the pilgrims." So why do I find myself fascinated by him? Maybe it's because a lost soul is the best friend a body can have.

"I'm moving in tonight," Kent says. "Just thought I'd look around a bit more."

I smile, or try to, as his bright blue eyes zero in on mine.

"Sure. Fine. Welcome." Did that sound friendly? Why is he *still* looking into my eyes, even as he takes another drag? Finally I have to look away, my face flushing again for no reason. We're just a couple of guys having a conversation, no big deal. It happens all the time around here.

Except that it doesn't. Not like this. Even when I first met Todd and Davy and Aaron and Dwight, there was nothing like what I'm feeling now—as if I've not only *thought* of doing wrong, but have already done it.

Kent can see all of this in my eyes, I know it. But he only smokes, and stares, and reads me like the book I'm feigning interest in. It's time for another effort to make everything seem natural, but as seconds tick by the chance to redeem the moment moves at warp speed, out of sight. He crushes out his cigarette and says, "Okay, see you later...Paul? Is that right?" The door is about to close behind him when he pauses again. "Say, can I ask you something?"

To pose that question is *already* asking something, a pet peeve of mine. But I try to put on a bright smile. "Of course."

"That guy who left recently? Dwight?"

I don't know why, but his question disappoints me. I guess I expected something more personal. *"Six inches, Kent. Versatile, yes, extremely so. I swallow, too. Always have. In for a penny, in for a pound."* "What about Dwight?"

"Did you know him? I mean, did you get to know him before he left?"

Sucking Dwight's chest hair while he moans, polishing his off-center knob till he begs me to bring him off. "A little, I suppose." Enough to know that Dwight had a problem. Not that half the world isn't disturbed—no, three-quarters of the world, at least. With Dwight it was anger. *"We're all angry,"* I tell him, *though the anger that once motivated me was gone, leaving me hollow. I rock him in my arms as he cries.*

"I can't do this anymore," he says. "I can't, I can't."

"Baby, hush." I hold his scrotum, warm his balls in the palm of my hand. A final pearl of cum leaks from his slit. "You can do anything you want, I don't mind."

He nearly chokes on tears. "That's not what I mean!" Heaving himself up, he turns toward the door as if he might step out like this, naked and semi-erect, into the hallway. Instead he raises his pale fist and slams his knuckles into the wall. "Shit!"

"Baby, baby." Arms encircling him from behind, my fingertips soothing his tits. "Let me sell you a pardon. I'm the only one who can, you know...."

His fist slams the wall again. The ancient plaster crumbles, but that's not what I'm worried about. "Honey, don't," I tell him. "That's your jack-off hand, you don't want to..."

Kent's voice intrudes. He's still questioning me, but it's hard to follow. "Excuse me?" I ask.

"I asked you if you saw him leave the house. Dwight."

"I don't see..."

"On the day he left. Did you actually see him go?"

"Well, no, I don't think I did." Actually I know I didn't. No one did, we didn't even know he was gone till Brian announced it at breakfast. "Why do you ask?"

"Oh, no reason."

As if such a question could fail to have a reason. I'd sneer at him if he wasn't so cute, standing there with his little package pointed at me. *"Mind if I ask you a question, Kent?" "Why, not at all. Eight inches. Get your trick towel ready, I blow a wad like you've never seen. But you have to fuck me for a good hour first."*

"Okay," he says. "Okay, Paul. See you later."

Kent's officially moved in now, making five of us instead of four, and relieving me of the duty of being The New Guy. He hasn't taken to wearing sweatpants yet; he showed up at breakfast in the tight jeans I first saw him in, walking like a guy who's saddle-sore, picking delicately at his crotch when he thought we weren't looking. He held his hand over his glass, refusing juice, and I was thinking, *Drink, man, you must be dehydrated.* Over the past few days he's been practicing the ritual masturbation, the purging of seed that's meant to mark our first days here. *Kathwacka thwacka thwacka* goes his headboard against my wall, and I'm thinking, *Good Christ, he's making enough noise for two rutting wildcats.* But at least he's doing it in bed instead of jizzing all over the room.

Now the two of us are in the den, and he's easing himself into an armchair. If he were naked... I'm picturing a trim torso, with enough definition to make it memorable. Big, sensitive nipples—why not?—and a mischievous furrow of hair leading from his pecs down to his navel, picking up again in a beeline to his bush—a creeping Charlie. Yeah, they call it a treasure trail, too, or a nature trail, but creeping Charlie is the name I prefer, I don't know why. Oh yes, he's definitely sore, not quite daring to cross his legs, the tender rim of his German helmet probably chafed, and I'm sending him advice, telepathically. *More lube, plenty of it. And look into some sweatpants. Please.*

"So," I ask him, "how are you settling in?"

He winces, shifting to get his cigarettes from his pocket. The one he shakes loose is curved like a half-erection. He lights it, takes a drag, lets it out. Picks a fleck of tobacco from his tongue. "Did you feel funny," he asks, "when you first came here?"

"I feel funny every day," I tell him, trying to suppress a laugh. Just then I catch, even through the combined smoke of our cigarettes, the slightly brackish scent of male skin and seed.

Maybe that house rule is wrong, the one about no cologne or scented aftershave. There are more seductive aromas by far. As my nostrils dilate I ask him, "How do *you* feel funny?"

He shivers, as from a sudden chill. "Oh, it's nothing." He hugs his upper arms, briefly buries his nose in the fuzz of his forearms. "I just wonder if everything here really is the way it seems."

Okay, so he's figured me out. He's read my thoughts. He knows I've stripped him naked. *Suddenly his eyes lock onto mine. "I can't self-suck anymore," he says.*

"Beg pardon?"

"I used to be able to self-suck."

"I've seen pictures of that. It looks awkward."

"No, man, it's a trip, sucking yourself off! You ever try it?"

"Well, this is probably the kind of thing where size matters, and since I can barely find my dick with both hands...."

"I'm just not that limber anymore. It ain't fair." He gets out of his chair, pulls up his T-shirt with one hand and shoves the other down the front of his pants. I was right, gratifyingly so, about the creeping Charlie. "Shit, I'm getting hard again, just thinking about it."

Okay, it would be hot to suck yourself off. Never mind how you'd look, curled up like a caterpillar that's been poked with a stick. And not to be able to do it anymore... I slide forward in my chair. "Bring it over here."

The quickest decisions men make have to do with sex; you can measure them in nanoseconds. He pulls out his double handful of dick, and I see how chafed he is, poor thing. This calls for great delicacy, and a mouth that's less dry than mine at the moment. I raise my coffee cup and take a mouthful—a funky rinse if ever there was one, but it's not like I'm trying to kill germs. Kent walks over, his engorging dick reaching me l-o-o-o-n-g *before the rest of him does. I take a firm grip on his asscheeks, guide him in. This is what he needs, a wet (who cares if it's coffee) mouth that knows how to suck. His knees buckle, he damn near falls on top of me but I'm with him, sliding down so he can brace his hands against the back of the overstuffed chair. Now I'm the one who's nearly curled up like a caterpillar, but who gives a fuck, I've got dick in my mouth, a real lip-stretcher, and the smell of his bush up my nose. My left hand encircles his balls as my right grips the length of shaft that won't fit in my mouth. He tastes, not surprisingly, like the sea—the brine and mucus of that life-giving stew. I expect a small, dry load, the kind you get in the morning from a guy who's been coming all night. But* whoosh, *he's gushing, my mouth brimming with incoming tide.*

"Holy fuck," *he says.* "That was great."

Wiping my chin, I look up at him. "Okay, so now you know. I'll never be an ex-queer."

He puts himself back together, handling his privates as if they're made of glass. "So fucking what?" *Unsmiling, he winks at me.* "There's no such thing as an ex-queer."

THE SHIFT

Joe Birdsong

Thursday, November 29, 2001 (Thanksgiving)

'm in a dive bar in New York City. It's called The Hole, and it's located next to what used to be a funeral home in the East Village. The city is still reeling from the disaster of two-and-a-half months ago. As I walk down the street, the twin towers reflect back out of every set of eyes. Giuliani is finally leaving office. Residents are starved for distraction, exhausted from the trauma that now seems to be synonymous with *New Yorker*. We are hungry for a return to the days of grit, for our concrete jungle to be returned to us as the uninhibited playground that is now legend. Each week Dean and Jonny throw a party that serves this end. It is for the dirty, hungry, horny men and boys of New York. These two empress-arios transform this dump, The Hole, into the sleaziest, sexiest, most delectably decadent den of iniquity, and call it *XXX Thursdays*. It is a weekly revolt against the atrocities that have been hurled at us, with venom, from Gracie Mansion.

I've been working at this bar each week for the past month. The job is extremely precise in its intent: maintain the go-go! Maintain? Indeed. An enviable position, in which I get paid to do the following: fetch the boys their drinks, so they do not parch; feed them their little blue diamond-shaped Viagra pills, so they are confident; if they are new to the party, introduce them to the principals, and give them the tour; most important-ly, watch over the boys, protect them from disorderly patrons. The incident that bore out the need for this newly created job involved a drunken, or perhaps sadistic, guest who attempted to set fire to an entertainer's ass. My tasks are a delight. I enthu-siastically understand that satisfied entertainers equal satisfied customers. This squadron of XXX dancers will evolve over the next year into what will come to be known as Mr. Joe's XXX Go-Go Patrol. Tonight, however, we are featuring a different crew, a special holiday treat provided to us by Rentboy.com.

I arrive at work after a particularly unsatisfying holiday. It is way too cold. I've had the obligatory dinner with friends who coaxed me out of my apartment that afternoon. I've just left Frank at Café Pick-Me-Up on Avenue A. I'm really on edge. Damn everyone and his holiday cheer.

Our typically well-attended party is about to burst at its seams, this being a holiday night. So many people are inside, I can't navigate comfortably. It takes me at least ten minutes to traverse one end of the bar to the other. A good sign of a success-ful night, to be sure, but it doesn't complement my sour mood. At around eleven-fifteen, I check my watch and think to myself that no one from our featured entertainment has arrived yet. Fifteen minutes later, I'm getting concerned. Still no entertain-ment. Midnight looms before us with no go-go. The open bar ends soon, the place is full of hungry, horny men and boys and the line stretches down the block and around 3rd Street. Dean tries to call the Rentboy.com booker. No answer. We try to call some of the guys from our regular crew, but of course no one is available. Exasperated, Dean looks at me and asks, "Wanna get naked?" As nonchalantly as if someone had just asked me to light a cigarette, the word *okay* comes out of my mouth.

Little do I realize what's about to take place. I've heard countless stories from people who have moments of truth, epiphanies, awakenings, or even "God Moments." What is unfolding before me is my God Moment. Mine happens to be a Go-Go God Moment.

There is no internal debate, no questioning. For reasons unknown to me, I simply answer, "Okay," and I act. A window is opening. Once I begin the process, it is no longer my decision. I'm on autopilot.

My life flashes before my eyes. Instances when I have acted out the bad boy role replay like home movies. Untold crimes against society (at times of a superhuman nature) played out in the relatively safe confines of backrooms, bar bathrooms, club dance floors, even in the streets, now kick-start a more public rebellion. The anonymity of these feats will no longer be factored into my equation. My history of sucking and fucking at the world now serves as a springboard to an arena of the unknown.

I carry these thoughts with me as I make my way down the back hallway. I pop a Viagra, and climb the ladder to the dirty candlelit hayloft that serves as a changing room. I strip down to my underwear and begin to stroke my cock, as I wait for the pill to kick in. At first I play with myself gently. Then, I stroke myself a little harder. Where's that lube? There it is. That'll help, I think, as I pour the grease into my hand, and I rub myself up and down, pinch my nipples, rub my chest, fondle my balls. My cock is stiffening. The problem is I have too much time to think while I'm waiting to get fully erect. I wonder if my cock is big enough. My body really isn't that great. I can't even dance that well. Stop thinking so much! Focus! Focus! This is about sex, and sexual freedom. It's a political act! That's what it is! Stop the oppression!

The music is loud, raucous rock 'n' roll, courtesy of DJ Lily of the Valley. This will be perfect—she plays all my favorite music. She's calling to me from the main room. And so I climb down the ladder and push my way through the throngs of men lining the dark hallway, making my way toward the light. I step up and onto the stage, my fully engorged dick ready to be worshipped.

As I stand there, it never occurs to me that someone else is now driving this experience and I'm just along for the ride. The only direction I know is that of the music. The lights are pulsating and flashing. Luckily, I can't see anything, save for the faces directly in front of the stage. I know now, however, that the jig is up. And so I dance and writhe and cavort and tease, and from that stage I am fucking each and every person in the room. Suddenly, I am the star of my own Self, and there is no stopping me. I taunt. I tease. I rock. I roll. Hundreds of men dance in front of me. Many approach me; reach up to me; rub my legs, my stomach, my thighs, my crotch. They slide money up and down my body, pushing it into my underwear as they cop a feel. The more I give, the more they give back. Finally, I slide my underwear down to the floor, step out, and I am free.

Time and space are no longer variables. I cannot say how long I've been dancing, or how many times hot sweaty men caress my ass, play with my nipples, and take my cock into their mouths underneath the strobe lights. This is what I know: I have been lifted high with an unbridled fervor. I have been carried to another dimension, one where man lives without constraint. And I have a soundtrack of heroes directing the journey: Blondie, Bowie, Queen, Sex Pistols, Siouxsie Sioux, Culture Club, Beastie Boys, Nirvana, Beck. They have always been with me, and now we work in tandem. Every triumph and every tragedy has led up to this moment. Courage. Fear. Vanity. Shame. Passion. Trepidation. Joy. Horror. Ecstasy. Tonight, I honor them all, as my shadow comes into my light.

It is in this experience that the full meaning of oppression reveals itself to me. It is as full and clear as the word *freedom*. Centuries of so-called culture and sophistication have brainwashed me. An imprint surfaces, and it is the tribal ghost dance of my ancestors who danced for guidance and for healing the spirit. I commune with my innermost Self, only to discover I have lit a match, and I see myself naked. There is a part of my soul (that is, my shadow) that has remained dark, in the dark. Now, I celebrate that darkness. This, my friends, is what I call the Shift.

Historically, I am a self-identified lurker. I am attracted to the night, to watching the stage from the audience, and to art. I approach it, I applaud it, I give it money, and I report on it to others. I dance around it. Now, however, this thing has occurred. The Shift. Once I engage it, I must continue. Once an idea presents itself, I must pick it up, feel it, smell it, taste it, and live it. Today, that is my only option. For what is the opposite of living? Dying. Killing.

The fact that my God Moment involves my having sex with hot, lusty men in front of hundreds of people, dancing and reveling to my favorite music, is not something I take lightly. It is poetry. Jungian analyst Robert A. Johnson describes it in this way: "Great poetry makes these leaps and unites the beauty and the terror of existence. It has the ability to surprise, and shock—to remind us that there are links between the things we have always thought of as opposites. It is whole-making and thus holy, and the most important experience of a lifetime."

THE END

James Williams

They say these are like opinions because everybody has one, but Stevie's was so eloquent as to be a point of fact. More than that, it was the art he built his life around, at least as far as I was concerned. He used to get dressed up every now and then for any and every reason, but he almost always went out on a limb on Friday afternoons. When I came home from work he'd greet me like some barefoot Chippendale in tuxedo pants and bowtie collar, or a bristly, pneumatic hunk out of Tom of Finland; other times he'd show up at the door in hot pink deep-cleavage Spandex tank top tights, with or without a crinoline tutu. But whatever seriously grandiose sort of costume Stevie did on any particular day, he never liked to hide his chest.

Stevie's chest was sculpted like a young god's, curved in graceful planetary arches that rose like bridges crossing mountains, with milk-white arabesques of blue-veined marble set between shoulders of monumental granite, tapering to a waist I could easily have held if I had three hands, rippling like a school of fish in a tidal wave or like a dozen quivering loaves of fresh-baked pudding. His slim hips seemed to fade away from there, which made no sense at all atop his tree-trunk legs, yet there he was: cool and hot, chiseled and cuddly, firm and gentle, sweet and severe, perfectly proportioned like a 1940s cartoon of a he-man. He was my yab-yum, my juicy Lucy, my holy heavenly hunk-o'-honey, and I was the man he loved.

Not to say I didn't love him back, I did, and not just for his physical magnificence; but we always had different agendas. In between those Dawn Redwood lower limbs he tucked not just a dick as big—to borrow part of Lenny Bruce's famous *mot*—as a baby's arm, but also, right behind, a pair of cheeks like boneless fresh-dressed roasting turkeys. Oh, my: first I think of him as art, then elements of earth, then in the original noir humorist's imagery, then in metaphors of food…. And even if he was never quite simply human to me, food was certainly one of his advertised delights. Those evenings he greeted me in the least elementary drag he also set before me the greatest alimentary de-lights, which he had prepared, I came to think, in order to watch with fascinated horror the gustatory pleasures I expressed. He brought forth from the kitchen large roasts studded with rare fruits and spices, pungent birds and fish and cutlets grilled crisp on the outside and soft on the inside, toothsome grains and roots paired up as if for marriage with amendments made from their own juices, exotic pastel custards, sculpted vegetables intertwined with the opposites they attracted, buttered sauces savory and sweet, pastries puffed and tarts tatin'd; and while I ate he sat before me with his great, bare chest exposed; both massive, muscled breasts tripling the space they occupied when-ever he raised his thigh-like arms to sip the steaming bowls of unadulterated, filtered, re-evaporated water he held to his face cupped in his plate-sized hands, watching me through the fog he turned into a misty curtain every time he exhaled.

Food was a stratagem for Stevie, as costume was another, and as his magnificent physique may have even been a third. I'd put nothing past him. And why would anyone as sumptuous as he go to all these troubles for a live-in boyfriend when the troubles themselves would warrant their own worth? Because, I think, of what he really cared for.

Dinner over—or my dinner, anyway, since it has always been hard for me to believe he actually survived on the hot water that was all I ever saw him consume—and the food preparations somehow miraculously dispensed with even before I had come home, Stevie left the dishes for some hour when I was asleep or away, and came to sit in my lap. "Came to sit in my lap" is all the truth of it, but wholly apart from the disparity in our sizes— Stevie towered over me when we both stood, was broad enough to shield me altogether from the sun, and weighed nearly twice what I did—the phrase doesn't begin to convey the dimensions of the fable. When Stevie saw or decided I had finished with my meal he had a slow, salacious way of taking his steam bowl in a single hand and lowering it toward the table surface as if it were a Stanley Kubrick spaceship moving with balletic precision toward its orbiting satellite port: the cream-white cup of buffalo china, or the near-translucent bone of Royal Dalton, or the painted and filigreed low-fired clay of some contemporary artist whose name would be traded for Picasso's in a quick year's time, would start to dance in the embrace of his palm-sized fingers, and the plants along the highboy, decanters in the china cabinet, the glittering crystal chandelier, the dust motes its light shone upon, and the very air itself became the background against which the piece of pottery moved hypnotic. But as I started to imagine I could even hear its music, the cup would softly come to rest on the jacquard tablecloth, and only then might I become aware that I had watched its whole descent, entranced, transfixed, mesmerized, while Stevie watched my captive eyes.

Eyes to eyes Stevie then stood up, transported as if in a single fluid motion from his chair. Considering his size, I found his composure and grace marvels to behold; there was never a moment in all the time I knew Stevie when I did not think he was well aware of the impression he made on me. The music I had thought so recently belonged to the floating, dancing, landing spacecraft of his bowl now seemed to occupy his own very specific movements. If he was wearing anything at all above his waist—the bowtie collar, the plunging tank top, a delicately gaudy rhinestone choker—he next removed that, pulling it the length of one sinuous arm and then the other with rapidly sinuous fingers all waving like leaves on a lengthy stalk of kelp in a languid Pacific lagoon; then he brought the isolated item down to the tabletop as if to land through water, where, effectively, it died. Whatever the piece of costume was it shone on him and then, apart from Stevie, it became just another discarded trifle no one had ever needed. His hands commanded everything as they roved across the landscape of his chest, or fluffed his feathered hair, or plucked a nonexistent nothing from before my vacant vision, but they never roved without a destination known and plotted to its last coordinate, and then they moved with just that same sort of certainty to whatever belt or thread of elastic held his bottom clothing up.

I never saw a pair of pants descend as slowly as Stevie's pants descended. It didn't matter if he was letting the crisp black tuxedo slacks slide so their bold satin stripe crinkled as it caught the sun or candlelight, or losing tights he had to peel away like Beulah skinning a summer grape, or pushing his legs free from tattered jeans with holes he could have stepped through, or dropping his drawers like a nighttime bathing suit in the moon-shine. First those huge hands and every finger on them would begin to wander as if they were blind and hungry and searching for his waist. They were on a highly coordinated mission from which no force on God's green earth could make them stray; yet always they seemed to have to seek that lean line out; always they seemed to have to make their ways from some far distant, civilized place across the mountains of his abs, down past the sultry valleys of his folded flesh, over his rivers and through his woods to the vast potential of his hot, humid, cloth-covered wilderness, where, by necessity and by design, they always managed to just stop short.

Some pants have belts and some have not; some have buttons and others do not; some zip and snap, some fold and tie, and some, even if they appear tight to the inexperienced eye, roll down easily as stockings off a close-shaved leg. Stevie let his fingers learn the nature of his pants each time, even if he had taken off the same pair every hour for a month. One finger might examine how the pants stayed up, while another began investigating how the closures worked this time; a third and fourth went off to learn how great was the expanse of pants, while a fifth remained aloof in case there was some call, unlikely as it seemed, to leave the pants in place a little longer.

"A little longer" is a phrase like "came to sit in my lap." A thousand simple words like these could never convey the story any better than a picture could. For Stevie "a little longer" lasted for whatever period of time felt right or otherwise served his purpose in the moment, and the length of a moment in which his purpose was served changed like any other chronological demarcation: *now* a moment was fast as a fleeing drop of mercury skittering away forever down the floorboards of a declined hall, *now* it moved as slowly as a glacier melting at thirty-three degrees Fahrenheit in a permanently frozen ice field.

As long as Stevie thought he still held my attention: that was how long "a little longer" lasted, and the nature of the pants had less to do with how time moved for him than with what he perceived of my desire. In that way I suppose I might conclude that I was the one who controlled the flow of time, I was the one who determined the length of *now*, I was the one who could decide exactly what "a little longer" meant. But that conclusion would be no more true than it would be true for a person in a car, scouring the densest section of a major metropolis for a single vacant, legal parking space where he could leave his car before a bus prevented him from reaching it; or some delivery van claimed it out from under him; or a utility truck usurped it with a ring of orange cones; or another driver, spinning on a dime, made a sideshow U-turn in front of a dozen Keystone Kops all falling all over their feet to get to lunch, jammed the bumpers fore and aft, and slammed his Hummer into the forlorn formerly compact spot—it would be no more true for me to claim that I decided the length of Stevie's *now* than it would be for that driver to believe that when, after a helpless hour of frustration, tears, and curses, his car skidded and stammered and stopped hopelessly jammed into a pothole from which it could not maybe ever be withdrawn and that happened to be right in front of his destination and that also happened to have a working meter waiting for his coin, he was actually responsible for the miracle: to just such a degree was I the captain of my fate with Stevie.

But like the hapless driver whose reward comes only from the virtue of apparent accident, so in the genuine fullness of time, each time the time would come when Stevie's fingers, for whatever reason, found the switch, popped the button, opened the snap, untied the knot, flipped the zipper, and !! just like that his pants were gone, and in their place there stood revealed in all its splendid sculpted glory the ithyphallic member men and women the wide world over would have fallen to their knees to praise and worship if they only knew they could. Was it like a baby's arm? It was like the cartoon spout of a cartoon sperm whale, rising from the sea floor, sending forth into the world the single source of the nexus lexis plexus of creation. If I had never raised my eyes from what was then displayed I could have been excused. If I had sat still gibbering in my chair no reasonable man could have possibly found my fault. If I had been struck deaf dumb crippled and blind, fallen off my rocker, fallen head over heels, flown to the moon and back, flown on the wings of song, flown with the wings of angels, died and risen from the dead, heard the voice of God and sung duets with Him, no one could have possibly imagined I had done anything he would not have done as well. Stevie had a beautiful dick. But he did not care about that at all.

Nor did he care about the Herculean balls he lugged about between those Douglas Fervent thighs he bared when all his pants fell down, though all the blessings, honor, glory, and power that belonged unto his dick most certainly belonged to them as well. But no: for Stevie all his costumes, all his cooking, all the stratagems of his musical, mystical body, all his hypnotizing actions and behaviors, all, all, all for him were nothing more than pre-foreplay, lead-ins to the final final act of finalé, the moment when climax changed to dénouement. All of everything he did was meant to lead us to the moment he desired, and wanted to remember.

Sure of my attention and certain I would go nowhere, holding my eyes with his until the entire weight of his turning head had to be precisely balanced on the single soft strand of his twisted spinal cord, slowly, slowly, like a liner out at sea,

Stevie turned his monolithic body around in front of me. His skin changed colors in every plane, each plane changed colors in every light, each light illuminated another carefully delineated muscle group and made him seem a holographic poster for the International Child. From his disappearing face in shadow deep below his sinewed neck; from his brawny football shoulders down his curling back and curving hips; from his wide, long thighs to his narrow, exquisite ankles; Stevie turned. He turned his side to me, he turned his back on me, he let me see the ripely rounded melons of his ass and then, only then, he peeked back at me across an abyss that seemed to grow from miles to years as, hopeful, shy, too eager not to let excitement show, he drew his hands back and took a pair of gracious grips on both his high, hard cheeks, bent just slightly at the waist, and millimeter by silly millimeter, spread himself apart.

I slipped off my chair as smooth as ice cream melting down a cone in hot July and threw myself across the scanty space that separated him from me. Kneeling, then, between the columns of his legs, looking up at the beach ball he had split apart, gazing through the blood-gauze curtain of his wondrous ball-filled sack to the living room beyond, I was, for these few minutes, king of all I beheld. This was why he'd buffed the body, made the food, worn the drag, studied me so carefully that he could hold me by the eyes while he took it off: so that if I were not yet smitten I would still be made to feel beholden to my fleshy icon, and give him in exchange this one thing he most desired. He thought that he had bought my love, and he felt he'd made a perfect bargain: he amused himself and me, and I rewarded him.

But I—I did not feel that I had paid when he performed his arts for me: instead I felt like a maestro's courted guest. I did not think that I had bought my Stevie's love or that mine had been bought by him, nor did I feel that I rewarded him when I heaved

up on his legs and threw him facedown upon the fainting couch
and plundered his hot hole with my hungry tongue. Instead I felt
I had seduced an idol, taken, for the price of feasting eyes and
belly lavishly, what other men would give their hearts to have.
I did think we had made a bargain, but I thought the bargain
went to me, especially since Stevie never for a single moment
failed to think the world resembled the precious image he had
made of it.

SLIPS

Rob Stephenson

You startle me when I turn on the light. You've caught me. You've been waiting there in the dark for me. You give me that face, the one full of despair underscored by your low harsh voice. You interrogate me without giving me a chance to answer. You are afraid of what I might say, but still you ask the questions. Under my baggy shirt, catastrophic drops run down from my armpits. You smell my fear. No, it's the odor of cigarette smoke from my clothes that's hitting you. Your words escalate in pitch. You want to hit back. You're wearing that silk slip with the lace fringe on the bottom. It's beige. It's tight. I can see your cleavage and the blue green veins that ride just under your pale skin. It's a composite of all the slips you've worn since I was a little boy, when you came into my room at night. The straps dig valleys into your shoulders. You sit with legs crossed on a reupholstered chair, one foot swaying back and forth as you berate me. This reminds me of the way your pinking shears open and shut as you cut along the black outlines of your dress patterns. All winter long you make awkward shapes on cheap yellow paper and pin it to brightly colored fabric. I envy the lovely, stringent designs dictated by the size and shape of your body. Now, your slip creeps up slowly, revealing varicose veins. They make a jagged blue music on the paper-white insides of your legs. You are still keeping time with your foot, but I hear a different beat. It's the ticking of the plastic windup timer on those Saturday afternoons in the kitchen alone with you. There's hot sugar in the air. I am standing too close to you, dropping glob after glob of chocolate chip cookie dough on stained metal trays. Maybe I'll get to lick the spoon.

You and your younger friends surround me as I walk home. You are by far the tallest of the five. There's no doubt that I'm an easy target. At this moment, I'm a ghostly white queer boy, high on god-knows-what. Your fist (dark brown skin on the outside, clenching, hiding the lighter skin of your palm) comes at my face and connects with my nose. You demand my wallet. I don't have one. I never carry one at night. My blood drips onto my jacket. You take the few wadded dollar bills I hand you and I start screaming. You flinch as awful words gush out of me. You expect me to be frightened, but I have had too much to drink. I am surprised by my outburst. You and the others run up the street. I stumble inside my apartment and start to shake. Now I am afraid of you. You must be seventeen at most. You are so beautiful. And you hit me hard. Could you ever imagine what it would be like if you touched me in a different way? Maybe you can't. Maybe if that happened, I would end up being the thief and you would be the victim.

You wouldn't do it for me at first, but eventually put it on after I insist. The beige silk stretches tight against your hips. Your chunky posterior pulls the slip up in back. I have you lying on your stomach on my king-sized bed. Or is it queen-sized? The tiny straps and the metal clasps cut into your shoulders. Every time you move you tear the seams out a little more along the sides. But you try to keep still for me. Your chalky skin takes on the shade of a Brazil nut's shell. My skin and the silk are bleached-teeth white. You push back against me and coax a few off-white pearls out of me. They bead up on the silk. You move again. The pearls smear and seep into the fabric. Then you stay still, trapped against me. I slap the side of your thigh. Kinky hairs poke through the worn material and tickle me as I glide up and down along the silken ravine you are offering. My hand continues to punish you and accuse you of imagined infidelities, encouraging them into existence. You know I want to make you feel good, but I don't think I could bear it if you were truly happy. So I shove my knee under the lace fringe and grind your testicles into the mattress. I'm still pressuring you to want to hit me back.

I tell you you're a no-talent bitch while I have you bent down over the arm of the sofa. It's become obvious that I need to be in control. But whose apartment is this anyway? Is it mine? I've never been able to afford a place like this. And it's so sterile you could lick clover honey off the floor. Maybe I should make you do that before the night is over. I can't believe how hard I am inside you. Your plump tits are so soft in my faggot hands. These are real tits, the kind that babies suck, just as big as on your album covers. I'm accustomed to the hard, flat kind. I can't imagine ever having received any sort of life-sustaining nourishment from sucking all those dry male nibs over the years. Maybe if they *had* offered up some for all that work, I wouldn't have turned to chewing them; pinching them; slapping them; making them burn, chafe, and bleed. But for now, I just like to squeeze your girly tits like water balloons on the hottest day in

August. I feel your hard nipples oozing their baby juice through the wet black silk onto my palms. I can't tell if I'm in an ass or a cunt. I'm too busy fucking, looking at the faint canary sheen of dimmed halogen spotlights on the black slip you're wearing.

You are downstairs making coffee. Many of your tastes still linger on my tongue. I steal the opportunity to peek into your closet. I'm immediately drawn to the crumpled pink slip on the floor, but there's something dark splattered on it. I'm hoping that it's paint. Why is it that everyone I end up going home with lately is unemployed? If this were the first floor, I would just hop out of the bedroom window right now. Instead, I pull out a glossy porn magazine from the short stack next to the slip. It has a caramel-colored guy on the cover, heavily retouched, pointing his special gift right at me. I look inside to see more pictures of him, maybe an asshole shot. But that's probably asking too much from this publication. I find the section featuring him, but all the pages are stuck together. I decide not to pull them apart and risk tearing them. I wonder how long ago you spewed your wad across these pages. Last week? Five years ago? I find a page that is not stuck to another one. On it, a darker-skinned boy sprawls with much less of everything to offer than the cover guy. There's a grayish powder in the crevice between the two pages. I touch it with my finger and consider wiping it on the slip. It's the ash from a lit and then forgotten cigarette that was dangling from your mouth. I see you naked, hunched directly over the photograph with your hands full, puffing away. I smell your smoky flannel bedsheets and suck the ash off my finger. I'm hard again.

You are onstage singing at a big club. Everyone stops danc-ing to watch you, waiting to see if you will live up to expecta-tions. You meet me backstage after your performance, after the fans have left. Your theatrical makeup makes you look clown-ish and in that formfitting outfit, your nipples look bigger than they are. I want to touch them, but they are sealed tight. Your clothes have become part of your skin. You kiss me. I taste your stage makeup; the powder sticks to my beard and I snort it up my nose. It numbs my gums and my tongue. I can't feel you anymore. I can't tell if I'm hard or not, but I follow you back to the apartment. Since I can't remove your clothes, I decide to wear the scarlet slip myself. I feel the silk caressing my torso, teasing my ass. I'm hard all right. And so are you. You make me lick your clothes all over. It's payback time. You smack me around with your big hands. I'm on my stomach, gasping for air. It would feel nice if I could cry. You ask me to describe what's in the picture on the wall above your bed, but I can't speak. You're lubing me up with fat fingers. I can't remember which apartment you mean, which bed, which picture. You're starting to slip that latex-covered, coal-black slab into me. I realize the picture above your bed is the same picture above every bed that I've ever fucked in and I've never turned on the light to look at it.

Ad libitum Da capo

KNIVES AND ROSES

Sean Meriwether

When your eyes close, that night slams into your mind. The skinny thug moving toward you, the gun in his hand quivering, *You fucking faggot*, a shot eclipsing all sound. Eyes open, the vision of him hangs sharply before you, a flash of light in a dark room. It never fades.

Your boyfriend, Richard, asks when you're going to let it go. *It's been three months*, he says. *I hate seeing you like this.* You close your eyes and turn away.

You're back behind the bar, the junkie with the gun rushes in the front door, chaotic energy jerking his sinewy limbs. The dark pistol vibrates as it rises to meet you. *Give me your cash.* A nervous laugh explodes from your throat. His pinched face sours and the gun connects with your head in a blinding tang. You drop to the dirty floor and he stands over you, larger than life. *Don't you fucking move.* You taste copper and snot and you don't move.

The kid bangs the cash register open and wads the cash into his fist, slams the fist into his pocket; an exaggerated turn, every muscle in his body moving, and the gun is inches from your throbbing face. *You fucking faggot*, he says. It echoes in your head, louder with each repetition, purging up memories of your high school locker room.

You avoid the dark orifice of the gun and study the tattoo scrawled across the chalky underbelly of his arm, a long blade inked from wrist to elbow swarmed by angry roses. Each rosebud is puckered like a virgin's asshole, and a slim blade projects beyond its tight lips—an orchestra of potential pain. The black lines are jagged, the red already fading. *Amateur*, you say to yourself. *Distinguishing feature to tell the police.* You have three seconds to study it before the blast knocks you back.

The gunshot is like the clap of huge hands; not loud enough to cause the spreading burn in your shoulder. You touch warmth with your opposite hand, your fingers come away red and sticky and you stare at them like you stared at the tattoo. *This is important*, you think. *I'm bleeding.* You look into his confused blue eyes—they'd be beautiful in another situation—and he says it again, *Faggot*.

Your eyes pop open and Richard is staring at you. He worries about what you're thinking. You tell him to leave you alone.

The police interviewed you in the hospital while you were hooked up to monitors that you could hear but can't see. You told the two cops about the tattoo, its image so clear in the blur of events that it took on surrealistic importance. The cops promised to catch and prosecute the punk bastard to the fullest extent of the law, but they were going to need your cooperation. They urged you to come down to the station and look at some pictures. One cop handed you a card and told you to call when you were ready.

You didn't tell them about *You fucking faggot.* You blamed it on the painkillers and the shock, but you knew the truth. You planned to tell the police the next morning, then when you got out of the hospital, then when you were looking at mug shots, but you never do tell them. You don't tell anyone.

The cops weren't optimistic as you poured over books of pictures that blended into the same face. Headshot, profile. Headshot, profile. Hundreds of criminals you realized were on the streets. None of them was your tattooed man. The police have no leads.

Richard turns all Oprah on you. He says, *You can't live your life as a victim. You have to take control of your life.* You tell him to shut up.

The tattoo comes alive in your dreams. The roses dart off the Medusa head of the knife and fly at you. You are frozen as the roseblades slice through your clothes, teasing your hot flesh with their pinpricks. You lie beneath the blue-eyed entity in the darkness as your mutilated clothes disintegrate. *Faggot,* he says. *You fucking faggot.* The knife rams your ass, holy and searing, until you are reshaped in its form. In his blue eyes you are his tattoo, swaddled in roses. You wake up in a cold sweat with a guilty hard-on and roll away from Richard's sleeping form.

You start drinking so you can sleep, then take over-the-counter sleeping pills, then prescriptions, but they only make you groggy and more depressed. You stop showering and dressing. The television is your only connection to the outside world. Richard says, *I can't watch you self-destruct. You need help.*

You agree to disagree. Richard moves in with his friend Cathy. The apartment is dead without him. You drink yourself into a stupor and wake up with your face in the toilet. *This can't go on,* you tell the soiled ceramic rim.

Going outside makes you vulnerable, the tattoo man might be around any corner, behind every tree, but you begin to realize you *want* to see him. Your alcohol-fucked mind cranks into gear with plans for capture. If the police can't find him, you will.

You hit the lowest local bars, slopping up cheap drafts while you attempt to private dick the bartenders. They eye you suspiciously; you don't belong in their world like the kid didn't belong in yours. No one knows the skinny guy with the knife and roses tattoo, but they always suggest another bar to check in.

Between bars you're drawn to street punks and hustlers, boys who claim to be straight but jerk off for twenty dollars while you watch. You pick the ones with tattoos; they sit in the passenger seat of your car and pull on their soft cocks, talking big. You ask to see their tattoos, their malnourished flesh graphed with black lines and curves, skulls and Virgin Marys, knives and roses. You touch these marks, when they let you, tracing a map to him. *He's here*, you whisper.

The hustlers send you to tattoo parlors, which are secreted in rundown houses, crowded trailers, and the back rooms of bars. You tell them who you're looking for, describe the swirl of roses surrounding the knife, even sketch it from memory, but they can't help you. *The kid probably did it himself*, they say.

Richard is in your apartment when you come home one night. *It happened months ago. Why can't you just let it go and move on with your life?* You tell him to fuck off and throw him out.

Richard will never understand how the tattooed man changed you; he gave you a mirror to your true self. You want to go back and fight him, do something instead of sit inertly on the floor, but you can't change the past or yourself. You swallow *faggot* until it fills the hole inside you with noise.

You pick up a gun in a pawnshop downtown. Its weight is comforting in your hand and you are energized by the black metal, as if it held a charge. You pace the apartment knocking off visions of the tattooed man with pretend potshots, *Pow-pow*.

The nightly dreams begin to fray; you are no longer paralyzed beneath him. You lunge out of the way in time, pushing him down with your feet. You knock the gun from his hand and turn it on him. You grab his loose jeans, yanking them down and exposing his hard cock, and he's crying, *Please do it.* Your sleeping mouth explodes with the salty taste of him.

Lying awake in bed you draft a revenge fantasy. The gun is in your hand, the rose and knife tattoo inked across your arm. He's huddled on the floor, completely under your control. You say, *Suck my cock.* He fights you with his eyes, but his mouth complies. You tell him to bend over, *faggot*, and he angles his lanky frame over the bar, exposing the moist pucker of his asshole. You open him up and fuck him, beating him with your cock. Each thrust is pleasure and payback. The tattoo on your arm swirls out to inscribe both of you, burning across your flesh like fire, until the knife is you, the rose him. You shoot into your fist as you imagine exploding in his crack.

The sketch of the tattoo is propped next to you as the ink artist rivets it into your flesh. You study the image that takes shape on your forearm, insisting that the lines be jagged instead of smooth, the red faded instead of full. He says, *It's your arm.* The knife extends from your wrist to your elbow. The roseblades blossom across your skin, their puckered tips ripe with potential pain. It takes four excruciating hours, but the pain absolves you, you squint out the first tears you've shed in a year, then cry openly as the ink artist bends to his work without a word. *He called me a faggot,* you tell him. The man doesn't respond.

You're a walking oxymoron, you joke, an empowered gun-toting *faggot,* the tattoo still raw and flushed with blood. You lodge the .38 in the front of your jeans, a second cock, and swagger outside, back to the bar where it all started. It feels like an exact replica of the original scene. The bar is deserted except for the new bartender, a comforting bald guy who looks like a listener. You aren't there to talk.

Richard meets you there at your request. He stares suspiciously at your bloodied tattoo, then at the gun as you lay it on the table between you. He tells you to put the gun away, but you pick it up and point it at him, staring down the barrel at his wounded brown eyes. *I want you to understand,* you say.

You order him to get behind the bar. The bald bartender tells you to calm down, though you're not nervous. You control the two men with the gun in your hand and think, *This is what he felt like.* You've never been harder in your life.

Give me your cash. Nothing happens. *Now.*

Richard moves toward you with an assurance that humbles and demeans you. You turn the gun on him alone. *Don't you fucking move,* you say. He keeps coming. *Stop, faggot,* you cry.

Two muted bangs overlap; the gun in your hand jerks as a bullet speeds past Richard, a spike burns into your forearm and the .38 goes flying. Richard runs to your side as you stumble forward, staring at the black pucker that mars your new tattoo. The bartender holds his gun on you and orders you both out of the bar.

Richard helps you to a chair and demands that the bartender call 911. His composure in the face of your downfall is humiliating. You want to hurt him as much as you want to be him.

Richard holds you as you cry into his shoulder, his body shifts to accept yours in the old familiar way. He tells you everything will be all right in soothing tones. You want to believe him, but the blue eyes of the tattooed man stare at you from the bloody wound in your arm; he is the knife; you, the rose.

YOU'VE HEARD OF IT

Vincent Kovar

So I'm in New York. I'm in New York and I am staying in a penthouse apartment overlooking a famous square. Everyone I know in New York lives in a penthouse, or at least a top-floor loft. That's not normal or at least it's not normal for other people. It's normal for me.

We are coming back from the dance club, the one below midtown, in Chelsea. You've heard of it. You've seen the T-shirts. You've watched the advertisements flash across the banners of the online gay sites. It's eight in the morning. We shut down the club because my friend, the one I am with, is a DJ, and we flew in just so he could play that night. Play that late night. Play that morning. My friend, the DJ, is very good. You've heard of him. If you haven't, you aren't somebody that hears about things. He flies to Amsterdam, Brussels, Tokyo, and all over the United States. He promises to take me with him. He won't. I already know he's lying. He doesn't.

We are both kind of high, me not as much; I spent the last few hours of the night making out with a young black man from Long Island. You haven't heard of him. I spent the last few hours making out with him on the dance floor where he begged me to have sex in Central Park. I didn't. Instead, we, my DJ friend and I, are walking down the sidewalk on a sunny Saturday morning in New York. It is beautiful. It is quiet. The street vendors haven't uncovered their tables. They haven't uncovered the old Stephen King novels, the battered LP records, the tattered pornographic magazines that smell of mildew and stale cigarette smoke. They haven't yet; they still sit, napping.

We walk back to the penthouse and go up in the elevator. As we ride, the doorman tells us there are guests upstairs. Everyone talks in the elevators. They say things that register in the doorman's eyes. It would make me laugh but I don't. He would laugh but he doesn't.

The foyer is quiet and I walk through the living room to the guest bedroom, the room where the DJ and I are staying, sleeping in the same bed. He snores and hogs the blankets and can't sleep without a fan blowing. We bought the fan the night before, downstairs in the drugstore. He pretends he doesn't think he's in love with me. I pretend not to notice because I already know he isn't. I know but he doesn't.

The owner of the penthouse is naked in the guestroom when I walk in. There is another man there I don't recognize. He is a porn star. You've heard of him. Almost everyone who hears about gay porn stars has heard of him. Everyone but me.

I can't tell if they were fucking or sucking or just rolling around. I stand stupidly at the door and stare at the tangle of muscled arms, muscled legs, shaved torsos, and bobbing dicks. I say, "Excuse me," and leave, walking back across the living room to the wood-paneled library where I slide the pocket doors shut.

I turn to the DJ. His eyes are shining bright with cocaine. So are mine. We bought it the night before from a man on the street and it isn't bad, considering. The DJ took most of it, in the back room behind the booth in the club. I had some too, not as much. I was off kissing the man from Long Island. I was hard against his thigh on the dance floor.

Behind me, the doors slide back into the walls and the owner comes in wearing a pair of tiny white underwear. I wonder why he put them on. The porn star, you've heard of him, is still naked and has a British accent. He's beginning to look familiar.

The DJ keeps asking, "Do you know who this is? Do you know who this is?" as if I am someone that doesn't know anyone. As if everyone I know in New York doesn't live in a penthouse. As if he is not going to take me with him to London and Miami and San Diego. He still thinks he is. He still thinks he is in love with me. I know the truth and we pour out more cocaine, including the stash I put aside in the guest room, the room where they were fucking. It is almost eight-thirty now and I can see the sun outside the stained-glass window.

I say, "Of course, I've *appreciated* your work," with an extra layer of innuendo on "appreciated." Maybe I sound sarcastic or maybe I sound witty. They don't care. Our eyes are shining with cocaine. No one has a straw. No one has a dollar bill. The maid won't be coming in today to make the coffee or restock the kitchen that no one uses. The owner takes a book off the shelf. It's *Hannibal,* the one about Hannibal Lector. The one after *The Silence of the Lambs.* Or is it before? He tears out pages and we use them to snort up the lines of white powder that we all take out from nowhere in particular.

The porn star is already on an alphabet of drugs. You've heard of them. The owner too, though his boyfriend asleep in the master bedroom pretends not to like them. This place, this penthouse, is where the previous boyfriend died. You've heard of him. You've read about it. The furniture is still the same. I sat in the room the day before and watched their eyes as they showed me the drawer where they keep the arsenal of dildos.

From behind other books comes a crystal vase filled with psychedelic mushrooms. I have never tried them. The porn star is playing his CD for us. You haven't heard it. He is trying to convince the DJ he should remix it, should make a club version of it. You haven't heard of it. You won't. The CD is terrible. Even stoned. Even with my eyes shining and covered in the liquid, imaginary mercury of cocaine.

I will try to convince the DJ to remix it anyway; try to convince him that it will be a triumph of irony. Later we laugh about this until people in Manhattan look at us funny on the sidewalk. They don't know who we're talking about.

But that night, that night the owner goes to bed, back to bed and his boyfriend, with the narcotic sweat of the porn star still on him. I wonder what it would be like for them, what it would be like a dozen floors down. What it would be like if no one had heard of them and if the sheets had a lower thread count.

The other man, the one who used to live here, died of a GHB overdose. Our host is the dead man's boyfriend. The late man's boyfriend gives me glasses of juice and tells me to give them to the DJ and the porn star. "Be careful," he tells me, "these have G in them." I remember the man who died but I carry the glasses anyway; carry them to people you've heard of. No one has heard of me.

The porn star bores me. His eyes are shining but dully, like a puddle on the sidewalk, a leaden gleaming rainbow of oil and dirt. He talks incessantly about his album, about performing it naked onstage while holding hands with a woman. He talks about the rich men who brought him to New York, the men who pay. He talks like a man still charming, like someone people have heard of, someone people pray to in temples lit by video. I go to bed.

The DJ acts like he wants me to stay. Maybe he is afraid that if I go the porn star will leave too. Maybe he hopes the porn star will make me horny enough to fuck them both. I go to bed and fall asleep in my jeans with my belt cinched tight around my waist. I go to bed acres above the street, windows open onto the square and the angelic horns of the cabs far below.

I wake some march of minutes later. I wake with the porn star's limp penis pressed against the side of my face. It is cold and heavy. He is trying to press it into my mouth. I am awake and asleep. I am scared like an animal caught napping and I am angry enough to throw these pounds of man, this worn object of despairing worship, off the balcony into the cement pandemonium of fallen angels below. "You're so beautiful," he whispers, and then repeats it. Then he tells me, "Everyone wants me to fuck them because I have such a big dick," you've seen it, you've seen his dick, "but I really want to bottom for you. I want you to fuck me."

It is the voice of God to men alone in the dark. To young men cowering in video booths; to old men alone in their apartments. But this man, this porn star you've heard of, is the answer to their prayers, not mine, or at least not mine remembered. Have I seen him? Have I stroked myself fiercely to his image? Remote control in left hand, cock in my right? Have I wished for him to come to me in the barn? In the prison? In the locker room?

My friend, the DJ, comes into the room and pulls the porn star away, the porn star with rug burns on his elbows and knees. The DJ shines his eyes into me and says, "This is a once in a lifetime chance. I have to. This is a once in a lifetime chance." And I feel pity for them both. I feel pity because they talk like people no one has heard of, like each is unworthy of the other and it is only I, in my disdain, who can touch them.

I caress the edge of sleep again, fist knotted around belt buckle; sex defended by denim armor, rivets, and leather. I caress the edge of sleep with my tongue counting my teeth. He slices into the tender flesh of sleep with the tip of a pen, the porn star. I think he is crying now but am not sure, am not sure I want to shine through the dark to care.

He shows me my own arm, what he has written there, and asks me to read out what I see. It is hieroglyphs. It is cuneiform. It is numbers. I say some of them out correctly but get others wrong. He writes his sevens with a cross through them, martyred in the European style. He writes them again, and again. On both arms, on my shoulder, on my back, and as I half roll over, on my clavicle. "You are so beautiful," he says again and again. "Call me. Call me."

His eyes no longer shine and I feel something for him. I feel the urge to lift him higher than where we are but there is no place higher than the penthouse, nowhere he has heard of. Can a lie be a gift? I lie. I say I'll call. I say I will to make the hurt in him a little less. Not because he expects me to call, not because he would actually answer, but because he wants me to want to call. The desire for desire. The dog chasing its tail. The Ouroboros devouring itself. The porn star so hung he can fuck himself into oblivion, where no one has heard of him.

He has consumed so many drugs he is foaming at the mouth, a foam of saliva and words. A foam of his father and his childhood. A foam of the rich men who call him across oceans to fuck but he goes down in the elevator anyway. He goes out into the morning below where the sun has only just touched and he carries some of the night down with him.

"It was a once in a lifetime chance," the DJ says to me again as he goes through his ritual before bed. We both know now that we will never love each other. We will never be that couple. That couple that flies from city to city. That couple of electronic beats and typed word. We will never be that couple you've heard of.

When he is asleep, I get up and shower. I wash away the sweat of the club, the press of transatlantic flesh, and I wash away the phone numbers men have prayed for. Even when I'm done, a few remain on the back of my left shoulder. Two or three digits surviving dimly, you'd know them if you saw them. A nine. A one, and a seven crucified by the line through its middle. The rest are just markings without meaning, broken, faded things no one will hear of.

I take a pillow and blanket out of the guest room, where the owner and the porn star greeted us with their fucking. I take the pillow and blanket across the living room where the carpets are scuffed with the marks of knees and hands and elbows. I go into the library where the porn star's CD has gone away with him and pages of *Hannibal* lie curled into tubes on the ottoman. The dark wood gleams like a polished coffin as the morning shines brightly through the stained glass, a funeral for no one we know.

I'm in New York. I'm in New York, eyes closing and the sun shining bright. None of it's normal. It's not normal for other people, though some of you might have heard about it, even if you haven't heard of me.

I'm in New York.

ARGENTINA

Richard Reitsma

When it rains, I think of you. Today, I'm obsessed enough to be out rowing in this not-quite-rain, not-yet-snow weather of late November in Michigan, the land of my exile. The misty breath rising from the river on a cold, rainy day like this reminds me of the unspeakable sweet nothings you once whispered in my ear.

My heart beats quicker at the thought of you, and I start to pull the oars through the water faster, past the Indian burial mounds, and on under the freeway. The early snow that only two days ago blanketed fall's decay is melting away, exposing the rotting corpse of a deer, mangled by a car. From the river I see a billboard asking me if I've *Got Milk?* Funny, that. Two days ago I had a good row in the falling snow. The billboard was blank then, the snow thick on the ground, the deer carcass and the Indian mounds merely silent bumps in the white landscape.

I opened the letter informing me of your death this morning. The note was brief, written in the unsteady hand of a poet whose fingers were smashed in payment for his supposedly seditious words. My friend, for whom every word is an agony, carefully wrote out your death sentence: *He who has touched us both too profoundly, has died, but not as we may have hoped.* It must have been the first time since our arrest that he's picked up a pen and put words to paper. I know for myself I never took another picture since that day; my mind is full of vivid memories, there is nothing I want a record of anymore.

I regret your being dead. It means I can never go back. Argentina is forever forbidden. How could I possibly go back after what happened between us?

I could always feel your presence in the room with me, no matter how dark the cell or how silent your breathing. It aroused me in impatience, and I would sweat as I do now.

That always amused you: my incapacity to control my body. You tormented me with it, knowing how I'd react to your proximity. You would keep me in suspense, allowing me to exhaust myself in furious anticipation and the desire for knowledge....

When anticipation became experience, my body quivered with painful realization. I writhed at your touch when it finally graced me, my body doing things with you of which it had never known itself capable. I've never been able to repeat those contortions that strained me to the limits of ecstasy: there's never been anyone else like you in my life.

So now when I think of all this, my flesh shivering with the memory of your warm caress, I manage a rueful smile, and laugh myself back into being, because I know you're dead.

Perhaps you thought I could save you? You punished me the way you wanted to be disciplined, because you saw evil in your desires. My body became the spoils of your war, your passions the victor, but you the victim: I was merely the territory of flesh upon which the battle was waged, and the war lost.

Argentina no longer means anything to me. You're gone, and everything I could possibly fear or love too much has vanished with you. I hated you, yet I had grown to love you: you were such a part of me that I had no choice but to learn to love you (revolting as that is to me) because I couldn't hate myself.

But loving you does not preclude attempts at vengeance and amputation. I would have liked to extract you like a molar and put you in a box, or cut you off like a gangrenous arm, stopping the bleeding with a smear of tar, like they do when tree limbs are sawed off. Then I could throw you away, forget you, and be gone and done with it, save for momentary phantom itches that can't be scratched. I am wrinkled and cavernous, porous like coral, attempting to fill my cavities with others. But like you, none of them stay.

Those who've spent long nights nestled with my body say that I talk in my sleep; that I make noises like a rutting pig. One even said he (or maybe it was she?) had seen strange markings well up on my flesh. At night, when I am not in control of forgetting, I dream of you. No one else has ever mattered so much to me. The indecipherable moans that come out muffled through the distant space of sleep are but faint echoes of the screams retched out in agony and hurled back to me from the walls of my cell, mocking my response to your fist, my blood, your boot, my blood. You cursed me for the blood, for staining your clothes and spotting your hands. My sanity grabbed, then, at some memory to escape the misery, and I remembered a portrayal of Lady Macbeth, hysterical at the sight of her stained hands....

I hated you less for the brutalizing of your hands than for my immobility. I hated you for tying my hands behind my back, to the chair. Did you know the rage and misery you caused my mind? It begged its body for protection, but the body failed, time after time, straining in fury until it surrendered to pain.

After you'd left, I would lick my wounds to gather back in as much of myself as I could. I felt then like a child, licking the trickle of blood and snot running from my broken nose. You robbed me of sight, my eyes puffed and sealed shut from too much blood, rendering me incapable of aiming my spit at you with any accuracy. But then, I could hardly spit: you saw to that the first day, giving me "lips like a nigger," as you laughingly told me. My hearing, the only sense with which you left me, was polluted beyond belief by the drunken whispers you planted in my ears. I could have closed my eyes so as not to look at you (your mustachioed sneer; the bulging, tattooed arms), but your fists swelled them shut. I could adjust to your pungent aroma of tobacco and sweat (produced by the effort of wanton rage?), but you broke my nose. I could have grown accustomed to the point of your leather boots kicking my stomach, my groin, my mouth, but the blow you gave my back subdued the rushing of sensory messages to my brain. So you left me with the one sense over which I could exercise no control, and you made my skin crawl, sweat, and stink as you filled my ears with poison, driving me to deadly madness.

Occasionally, the only soothing sound I heard, late at night, was the rain falling somewhere outside. One of my only memories of Argentina is that it is always raining.

I thought I could not desire death more at that moment. I thought I was dead, once, and decided it really wasn't so pleasant after all, if all it meant was that I felt the cold and misery and immobility of before. But then, at the moment of my despair, you introduced me to *el jefe,* your cock, your personal billy club, and I learned an agony worse than dying without faith in something: I met hope....

I was ready to confess to the crime, any crime, until that moment. After that encounter, hope grew at the possibility that perhaps you wanted me, you needed me. That gave me power, or so I hoped. But it didn't last long enough. You managed to deprive me of hope as well, your last revenge.

I had an adolescent fantasy involving Romans and triremes. It was a flexible fantasy that allowed me at times to be the plumed and bronze-breastplated centurion whose desire falls on a galley slave, captured from one of the Celtic tribes. At other times, I was the naked slave, painted in blue, eager for Roman conquest. Either way, *pax romana* was achieved in the post-coital embrace of bodies in my imagination. I used to masturbate to these ancient images, but I'd forgotten about them until I met you. I did not want to be conquered, but I desired peace, and my lust for my forgotten and vanished youth encouraged these thoughts from my latent pubescent mind.

I didn't know what you were going to do when first you cut me loose from the chair. I thought maybe you'd had enough of trying to get me to confess to espionage activities, and maybe you'd finally believed me when I said that I didn't honestly know what all this talk of spies and sedition was about. I don't know, anymore, what the truth was. Maybe I was a spy, a terrorist of images, working with my camera in collusion with the words of poetry scribbled by my friend. Would it satisfy anything if I were, indeed, an agent in the service of the CIA, the left, the right, or the middle? I'm no patriot. I pledge allegiance solely to the tribal markings that march across the landscape of my body. Did you ever really believe in the accusations leveled against me? I doubt it. Your obedience was to fear, desire, amorous loathing. Does it matter what you thought or what I might have been? I don't know if I care any longer. I only want to forget.

You laughed a slightly drunken laugh, which echoed a little

too loudly as you handled my weak-as-a-baby body, turning me
onto my stomach in order to tie my hands to the back legs of
the chair, where recently my ankles had been bound. It was a
source of glee for you to force my lips to kiss the spot where I
had stained the seat by defecating and pissing out of fright and
anguish: I admit I was not brave enough to control my bowels
or my bladder, especially after they'd met with the force of your
booted foot.

You told the others to leave, saying you had a sure method
to make me talk. And then you tore what little clothing I had
left intact off my body and, kneeling behind me, opened your fly
and shoved your cock into my ass, grunting your satisfaction.
I tried to scream at the first thrust, but shock overtook me. I
tried to ask you to spit on it, to make the going easier, but I only
made you laugh harder. What was omitted out of spite was ac-
complished with blood, and the pain subsided. Your whispered
words, used to incite a lover to orgasm, droned in my ears with
each digging thrust from behind as you grabbed my shoulders,
my waist, the legs of the chair to enter deeper and harder, attempting to produce the screams of pleasure or pain you heard
from your wife, your lover, your whore, your daughter, your
son, your mother....

I hated my responding erection. Despite myself, I was excited. But all the pleasure my traitorous flesh received was to be
slammed repeatedly against the seat of the chair with each pelvic
thrust from behind.

The iron closet echoed with the sound of your thrusts:
sweaty skins slamming against each other, the legs of the chair
scratching across the floor, your grunts from the effort of following a moving target. Then came the moan, and the shudder
of a momentary dying as you poured yourself into me, collaps-
ing, finally, on top of me. And then the silence of you pulsating,

shrinking slowly out of me. I felt your caress...or maybe it was a tired slap that my desperate mind read as a gentle lover's touch? And your gentle breathing, induced by postcoital bliss, intoxicating my mind, tickling my ear where your mouth rested.

It was the first time I had felt warm in days, and I did not want you to leave, despite the pain of your weight crushing my ribs against the edge of the chair so I could hardly breathe. I knew, finally, that I was indeed alive. I knew that everything that had preceded this moment, and everything that was to follow, operated out of your desire for me. Joy flooded my despair, and I knew you needed me. I no longer thought like a free man thinks, but like a slave, and the wild fantasy entered my mind that I could give you my ass and satiate your desire, and then the beatings would stop. The crescendo of my hopes came crashing down in a cacophony of confusion when you whispered, satisfied, "What a lousy fuck you are."

You had given, only to take away. You left, taking away my warmth, my hope. For the first time I cried, endlessly tearless wailing in the quiet of the afterglow, feeling nothing but the overwhelming desire to take a shit.

I never saw you again. The night after, someone else, with no less gentle hands, came in. I had expected others to follow behind you and fuck me. I waited for it for hours, but it didn't happen. You must have known that I was to be released, and so had desired to leave your mark tattooed indelibly in my flesh, so I wouldn't forget you for as long as I lived.

I have tried to purge your memory from my flesh with a multitude of lovers. Men and women have been used passionately to assuage my desire and my agony, but they are inevitably frightened away, rejected, disposed of. Some have tried to smooth out the rough topography of mountain ranges etched in my skin. Awkward kisses have suckled at the volcanic islands, burn marks from your cigarettes. Tears and unguents have attempted to burnish away the pockmarked territory, the no-man's-land of scars. But all expeditionary forces inevitably fail, incapable of deciphering the hieroglyphics of your conquest. My body is not a catalogue of heroic battle scars, but a crumpled cartography of humiliation that inevitably turns them away.

I had wanted to be the one to kill you: to strip you naked, admiring the powerful curves of the muscles that beat me, caressing the lance that invaded me; then, after assuring myself of your sobriety, to spread your legs and castrate you with a razor blade. I'd stuff your balls in your mouth, agape in terrified astonishment at my seductive revenge. Then, before you bled to death from that, stick a shotgun up your ass and feel the pleasure of it squeezing its load and shooting itself off inside your lovely body. If not me, I thought perhaps that privilege would be ordained for someone else, whose obsession was greater than mine, whose love for you matched the hatred enough to do it. Then, I thought, perhaps together we could rid you from our flesh; tear out the pregnant parts of our memories and lie together, sweat, cum, and blood mingled with tears; hold each other and forget, forever, and never rise from the bed of our protest.

But no. Revenge was not ordained, and I am angry, alone, cold, and wet. I cannot understand why you were allowed to die from a stroke while walking home one night in the rain, returning from the market in the company of your wife. You did not die alone, in agony. No, you stumbled, fell, and rested your body in a quietly expanding pool of spilled milk, until you closed your eyes, and left.

My body aches. I realize with a start that the current has carried me downriver. I am approaching the rapids, where I cannot navigate. Slowly, aching with every movement, I row the boat to shore, secure the bow, and climb up the muddy bank. I'll have to walk home now, get my car, and come back out here to get the boat. I am too tired, too cold, too lonely to row my way back upriver. I doubt anyone will stop along the freeway to pick me up, muddy and bloodied and wet as I am. I reach the road and realize there are few cars, the road is slick with ice, and it is so much colder now.

I doubt there is a silence vast enough to stop the screams, nor a cold deep enough to numb my memories, but still I search for it. I look up, wondering where the sun is, what time it might be, how long I'd been drifting. The rain has turned to sleet, stinging my face. I smile at the thought that it may yet snow today, enveloping everything in a vast horizon of empty white, covering my tracks, burying my boat. Cleansing, obliterating. Warm, soft, quiet snow...

I turn, and look back toward the river. The ice is gathering thick on the trees, outlining them in smoked glass. The ice crystals crunch under my feet, a delicious sound in the silence. The city is blurred from view, turning into a gray hill in the distance as the sleet falls with more intensity. I surprise myself, thinking: *This would make a beautiful photograph.* Perhaps. If only it would snow. As I walk, the sleet ceases. Silence. Then, slowly, it begins to snow.

BE CAREFUL WHAT YOU ASK FOR

Nick Alexander

The conversation drifts around France and the French. Jean and his identical clone partner, who amusingly turns out to be called John, take positions on either side of me, and chat. I can feel a move coming and I find the idea both amusing and enticing.

The two men are absurdly alike, and there's something quite exciting, in a freak show kind of way, about the idea of sleeping with them both, with their matching clipped hair, their identical little goatee beards.

By my third pint I am feeling amazingly relaxed, and the clones are standing either side of me, touching me regularly as they talk, a prod here, a playful punch there.

John tells me that they have been together for eleven years. I nod, impressed. "I don't know how you do it," I say.

Jean winks at me. "We'll show you if you want."

I laugh. "No, I mean how you've managed to stay together so long."

Jean smiles at me. "We'll show you if you want," he dead-pans. "The thing is to keep the sex life healthy. The rest fol-lows."

John leans in and says, "And our sex life is *very* healthy... with a little help from our friends."

"Here it comes," I think, and I wonder how I will reply.

"We have a great setup," Jean tells me with a salacious smile, adding in French, *"Notre cave est un veritable Disneyland"*— Our cellar is a veritable Disneyland.

"Hey! Why don't we go back and have a drink there now?" John says, feigning surprise at the idea that has supposedly just *popped* into his head.

I open my mouth to say, "Maybe another time."

But Jean interrupts. "It's nothing heavy you know.... It's only sex."

For some strange reason, that clinches it. It strikes me as the most honest statement of intent I have ever heard.

During the walk, the mirror-couple march either side of me.

I could feel as if I have a bodyguard, or perhaps as if I am surrounded, and in different circumstances that could be scary, or exciting. But the air of camp lingering behind every word is anything but virile, anything but scary.

Jean is telling me that the lounge still smells of paint, that they only just finished decorating it. John is interrupting him like an excited puppy to tell me that he chose all of the furnishings and made the curtains and cushion covers himself.

My fantasy world is evaporating fast.

The house is in the middle of an elegant two-story crescent. We climb the steps and as Jean opens the front door, John places a hand on my arse, pushing me across the threshold.

I bet that a few people have balked and run away at this point, not through fear but in sheer revulsion at the color of the room.

The curtains, heavy Dralon, are peach colored, as is the enormous sofa and the deep-pile, nylon, wall-to-wall carpet.

The cushions have been covered with thick canvas carrying an ethnic print. They would be tasteful were they not, also, peach.

"Sit there," Jean instructs me, pointing to the sofa.

John winks at me and says, "We'll be back in a jiffy."

I force a grin and sit in the sea of peach wondering just how long it is since I last heard the phrase, "Back in a jiffy."

The lounge has been knocked through to the dining room, which has the same color carpet and is filled by a glass and wrought iron dining table and chairs.

The bookcases contain sets of identical spines, which says more about misplaced ideas of interior design than culture, whilst the surfaces are occupied by a tidily arranged series of geometrically modern candleholders, vases, and paperweights: generic items from, I guess, Habitat or Ikea. Part of the sea of consumer junk that those stores throw at us every year, the same stuff people always seem to give me at Christmas and which I have to wait until springtime to bin.

When the twins return, their outfits, leather chaps, studded posing pouches, big motorcycle boots and harnesses, are so incongruous with the surroundings that it is as much as I can do not to snigger.

They sit either side of me and serve drinks from the bar, which for some reason has mock leaded windows.

"So what do you think?" asks Jean proudly.

"Yeah, great," I say, perusing the two.

If one can just ignore the fact that we're sitting in a sea of peach drinking sherry from a mock antique bar, the boys look pretty sexy, but truth be told, I'm having trouble ignoring.

"I'm glad you like it," John says. "It's always so nice when people appreciate all the hard work."

He plumps a cushion as he says this, and I assume he has misunderstood, as we are talking not about the room but about the outfits they have put on for my benefit.

But the couple, at least, seem in tune. "Took ages to choose the sofa though," Jean comments.

I think, *I can't do this.* I will make my excuses and leave.

"Time to take the prisoner downstairs I think," Jean says.

John stands. "Indeed," he agrees, knocking back his sherry.

"Look, guys," I say, as they each grab an elbow. "Maybe we can do the downstairs thing another time."

Jean laughs at me. "Relax, there's no pressure. Just come and look, you have to see our setup, we're not going to jump you or anything."

I'm intrigued by the mysterious "setup"—and they are entirely un-scary except in terms of their taste in furnishings—so I decide to go and see. Telling myself that I could probably take the two of them if I needed to, I follow John to the door under the stairs and then down into the barely lit cellar.

"Best room in the house," he says as he descends before me.

Jean rests a hand on my shoulders as he climbs down behind me.

The cellar is fabulous and I am truly dumbstruck. Were these not Mr. and Mr. Peach, I *would* be afraid.

The flickering light of fake torches dimly lights the rough stone walls. In the middle of the room, suspended from the ceiling is a complex set of pulleys and chains, the kind of thing you see in a *Kwik Fit* garage.

Along the wall is a huge tool rack containing a selection of toys worthy of any sex shop: clamps, rings, leather gear, hand-cuffs and a full set of dildos, laid out from small to large. The large one is, I note, *very* large. It all reminds me of my father's tool bench and spanner sets, and I briefly wonder if the one dildo the boys can never find is the one they need the most.

"Wow," I say, touching a hanging chain, "Dare I ask what all this is for?"

Jean laughs and slides a hand to my arse.

"If you want to know that, then you are obliged to partici-pate!" he laughs, his French accent suddenly quite strong.

I laugh nervously but pull gently away. "I'm not sure that right now is…"

"*Lache toi!*" he says. *Let yourself go….*

"It's just a new experience…."

"Yeah, but I'm not sure it's an experience I want to have," I say. "Not right now, anyway."

"Hey, why don't you just try on the gear and we'll show you how the pulley stuff works. You decide where you want to stop."

I look at the complex harness he is holding and remember when I was in New York years ago, remember saying no to ex-actly this. And I remember wondering a million times since, just what it would have been like.

I nod. "Looks like fun," I say. "Maybe I could just try the suspension thing? I mean just to see," I add. I can hear the dis-honest modesty in my own voice.

Jean winks at John who grins back.

A wave of heat ripples through my body, starting at my brow and sweeping down—a wave of panic.

John pulls my T-shirt over my head, and Jean moves behind me, takes my wrist and starts to buckle a heavy leather wrist-band around it.

"What's this?" he asks, running a finger along my scar.

"Bad car accident," I say, suddenly embarrassed.

"Don't blush," Jean says. "It's sexy."

"And no risks…," I say. "I'm HIV negative, okay?"

John crouches before me and starts to remove my trainers.

Jean, behind me, says, "You don't listen. We already agreed, no sex, nothing but suspension. Relax."

John removes the second trainer and simultaneously pulls down my jeans and my boxer shorts. My dick springs erect. I feel myself blush.

"Hmm, you're enjoying this, aren't you!" he laughs.

Jean leans around me and touches my dick.

"Hmmm, shame to put that to waste though," he says. They remove my jeans and clip identical restraints to my ankles, then John stands and lifts my arms. His partner, who has moved behind me, immediately clips the D-rings of the bracelets to two chains hanging from the ceiling.

As he tugs on the pulleys, stretching my arms taut, I start to feel fear again.

"Look…I'm not sure, actually, that I feel that comfortable with this whole…"

As I say this John clips my second foot to a floor chain, completely immobilizing me.

"Hey!" I say. "Is anyone listening to me?"

Jean speaks quietly into my right ear. "Just calm down, no one's doing anything you haven't given permission for, so relax and enjoy."

"But."

As I say this, in a surprise movement, he slaps my arse, hard. As I open my mouth to shout, he pulls a gag between my teeth.

"Ummm," I protest.

"Now shut up," he says. "And relax."

He buckles the gag behind my head.

I protest through my nose for a while but it only makes them laugh, so I give up.

Jean pulls a hood over me. I can still see through the eyeholes but my hearing becomes muffled. Images of the gimp in *Pulp Fiction* come to mind.

Obtusely, I think, *Thank god my mother can't see me now.*

As I protest and wriggle Jean says, "There's nothing you can do now, nothing you can say, so just relax, give in."

John stands up in front, strokes my dick very lightly and looks into my eyes.

Jean finishes lacing the hood and moves yet another chain into place, clipping it to a ring on the top, holding my head upright.

I hold my breath to listen to them speaking.

"...in a minute, once he relaxes...," I hear Jean say, "...he'll be begging...."

Then, one after the other, Jean clips patches across my eyes.

I hold my breath for a moment, considering the new leathery dark, and shift my weight, trying different ways to stand and hang on the wrist restraints. My heart is racing and I am sweating in fear.

At the same time, the taste of the leather gag, the smell of the hood, the very idea of my nakedness hanging before them, makes my dick stiffen.

Nothing happens for a while, and then I feel hands fastening a new series of straps around my legs.

A finger runs along the outline of the scar on my knee; they reposition the strap lower to avoid it. For some reason this attention to my needs reassures me. My heart starts to slow.

Someone reaches from behind and fastens straps around my waist and my torso, then around my neck and my waist.

The feeling of skin-on-skin contact is magnified in the

darkness. Just the simple feeling of their hands, the seemingly endless fiddling with straps and buckles, feels incredible.

Someone's leather sheathed leg brushes my dick and instinctively I writhe towards the contact. This elicits a laugh that penetrates the muffled silence.

For a while some complex operation of attaching goes on behind me. I can feel the four hands working simultaneously, connecting chains and ropes to rings on the straps, like they're doing some kind of puzzle, or macramé.

The process takes maybe ten minutes, though with only the sound of my breathing it becomes difficult to judge time.

Then suddenly the weight disappears from my feet and I start to float. The experience is amazing, truly out of body. With the weight distribution provided by the complex web of straps surrounding my body I don't feel suspended by any particular point, I just feel like I am floating.

I hear vague metallic noises through the hood and slowly I start to lean forward, to jerkily tilt. The movement continues until I am horizontal.

My legs slowly spread, I cannot resist, and some kind of pole or bar is clipped between them holding them wide apart. I can feel the cold air against my anus and I start to ache with the desire to be fucked.

I float like this for maybe five minutes, dimly aware of the couple moving around me, more and more obsessively aware of the state of my dick, hanging free, now hard, now soft, now hard again.

The dark isolation magnifies the desire for skin-to-skin contact to the point of madness. I feel as if I have taken Ecstasy.

I ache for more. My legs are wide open and my dick is pointing at the ground and I want more. I start to want *anything* as long as it's more. But nothing happens.

After a few minutes there is a jerky shifting in the chains connected to the hood and slowly my head lifts so that it is pointing forward.

In an unexpected movement that makes me judder in surprise, Jean rips off the eye patches.

"You okay in there?" he says, peering at me from mere inches away.

I nod as much as the restraints will allow.

John, who is out of sight, runs a finger along the crack of my arse as his partner leans into my ear and says, "You want more now?"

I arch against the finger as much as the straps will allow and make an *um* noise through my nose.

John laughs demonically and pulls Jean into view.

The two stand mere inches from my face and stare at each other.

They kiss, delicately at first, then deeply.

John runs his hands down over Jean's back to his arse, which is peeking pertly from his shiny chaps.

The two men kiss and stroke each other, pausing to play first with each other's nipples before moving lower to their pouches. They stroke and rub and caress each other through the leather, then unclip the pouches, revealing almost identical dicks.

In an attempt to generate some sensation in my own body I wriggle and writhe and am rewarded by the slightest sensation as my skin moves against the straps.

Mere inches from my suspended face, Jean rolls on a condom, turns John around, and slowly, sensuously, starts to lube his arse, forcing one, then two, then three fingers inside.

Occasionally John looks up at me, stares me straight in the eyes. His pupils are dilated and my dick twitches and judders in sympathy.

He says something, and I run the image of his moving lips through my mind. It's not hard to work out what he said.

"Fuck me."

Live porn. Never has my frustration felt more complete.

Jean slides his dick in, gently at first, maintaining his distance, avoiding inflicting the full length of his dick, but slowly he goes deeper and deeper.

He starts to pulls on John's harness as he pumps into him and their grunts get louder and start to pierce the material covering my ears.

As if I were a camera, they pause occasionally and change position so that I get a different view.

My dick jerks and judders again, uncontrollably. My arse trembles and twitches. Who ever would have thought being a truly passive observer could be so exciting?

The grunts and moans increase as they slam together, until, in a crescendo of slapping and pumping, tugging and shrieking, they come together, John's cum spurting onto the floor beneath my head.

I wiggle in my straps to remind them of my presence.

Jean pulls out and removes the condom, casting it into a bin, then turns toward me, standing before me.

He's standing so close that I can no longer see his head, only his groin, his glistening dick.

He reaches toward me and undoes two zips near my ears; the loudness of the zips after the silence is deafening.

He reaches for his dick, then wipes it back and forth across the gag covering my mouth.

"You want this now?" he asks, bending and peering into my eyes.

I nod and grunt.

He laughs.

"That," he says, "is how you turn someone into a sex slave."

John reappears at his side with the unfeasibly large dildo and hands it to Jean.

"You want this?" he asks.

To my shame, I nod and thrash, desperate for them to touch me, to release me from my enforced voyeurism.

Jean puts the dildo down on the workbench in front of me.

"Another time, maybe...," he says. "When you know what you want."

The two then move out of sight.

I remain suspended for what seems like quite a long time, maybe twenty minutes, but it's hard to say. Time moves slowly.

My state of arousal slowly fades to boredom, and my dick goes limp.

I make some groaning noises but no one responds.

I thrash around in protest and can hear the chains clinking, but nothing happens.

Just as I start to worry about getting home, just as I start to get angry, even a little scared, the chains and wheels start to clunk and shudder. My head starts to rise and my feet move hesitantly toward the ground.

As I am lowered, John removes first the hood, then the gag.

"Game over," he grins.

I take a deep breath of fresh air, and start to complain.

"Hey, what about me?" I say. "That's not fair!"

But John only laughs. "You need to be more careful what you ask for," he says. "Because round here you always get what you ask for, no more, no less."

LONESOME FOR OCTOBER

Steve Berman

After tearing open the glued seam of the large envelope and glimpsing what his uncle had sent him, Scott felt sure the old woman behind the counter of the campus post office had noticed the flush in his cheeks. He had come to consider any snail mail an unexpected treat, but what was inside was far better than cookies from home. He slipped the package under his arm and hurried off. Eagerness made the count of doors and floors to his dorm room seem endless. Alone at last, Scott let slip the calendar from the envelope onto his lap.

A neon pink Post-it note offered a belated *Happy Birthday* from his uncle. Beneath the shrink-wrap, which lasted only a minute in his hands before being ripped off and wadded up, a glossy monochrome brunet grinned as he buried another boy in the sand. Sunny lettering spelled out *Beached 2004–5* along the lower edge. He flipped through all sixteen months and could not find a single flawed guy.

Scott felt bad for poor September—blond, hiding his crotch behind a very phallic sandcastle—already last month's boy. But October offered a come-hither smile as he walked along the shoreline. He wore a thong that had slipped so low you could see the dark trace of pubic hair.

Idly adjusting his own crotch, Scott glanced at the clock. He had just enough time to dash off to the library and send an email thanks to his uncle before World Masterpieces began in the lecture hall.

Uncle must be psychic to have known exactly what Scott needed. Being the only gay guy in the suite—hell, probably the entire floor—left him the outsider. Having Grasky as a room-mate made matters worse. The only thing Scott knew for sure was that the guy seemed to enjoy just three things: eating cereal, avoiding washing anything, and making rude remarks.

Spite made Scott leave the calendar out atop his sheets. The dorm was small enough that Grasky could not help but notice, even if he kept to his half of the room. On his way out to class, Scott passed the doors of his other suitemates before lingering by the last one. Andre's door remained closed, as always. The memory of Andre coming into the suite, damp T-shirt and run-ning shorts clinging to his small but muscular frame, hadn't fad-ed since freshman orientation weekend a month earlier. Some nights he cursed his luck for not having Andre as his roommate, but constantly seeing such a hot guy might have been torturous. The boys on the calendar were teases enough.

When the dreams began, Scott naively blamed them on loneli-ness, anxiety, even a batch of bad Mexican leftovers he had found in the suite fridge. He couldn't recall many details, but when his alarm clock buzzed him awake, he found his boxers were clammy and sticky. He didn't think it right that he could be having wet dreams again; at thirteen, sure, but not in college.

Grasky had yet to complain much about the calendar, despite some sour looks. He did mention that Scott had been making weird sounds at night. Considering Grasky snored, there seemed little to say other than sorry, and the guy didn't seem to want that.

One night weeks later, Scott wondered what had woken him. One moment, he was on an abandoned Caribbean beach; the next, back in his dorm room. The gentle sound of the ocean was replaced by Grasky's labored breathing through his deviated septum. Mister October, the hot guy Scott had been holding hands with in the dream, straddled him.

The sudden realization that he was no longer alone in bed startled him so that he almost dislodged October. He gasped loudly then looked over in the direction of Grasky. But the room was so dark, he couldn't tell if he had woken his roommate.

A soft touch on his cheek turned his attention back to October. As his eyes adjusted, he saw that the calendar boy remained shades of black and white, as if the photographic image, not the model, was reality.

Scott blinked and tentatively reached out to brush his fingertips along the bare, muscular torso. The flesh felt satin smooth, too cool to the touch, but otherwise real. The boy had weight, pinning Scott down.

I'm still dreaming, he thought. *That's the only explanation.* He looked up at October's smile, the same he'd worn in his photo. *Well, this explains the wet dreams.* He chuckled at the thought.

With an uncanny ease, October slid the covers down, Scott's T-shirt up, and Scott's orange plaid boxers down. The calendar boy's face dipped and a slick cheek brushed against Scott's hard dick as he began kissing the insides of the freshman's thighs.

Scott squirmed and moaned. The kissing gave way to gentle nips of teeth and thrusts of tongue that touched closer and closer to where Scott really needed October to land.

"Please," he murmured, his hands slipping through calendar boy's hair, which felt like locks of spun glass.

October looked up from Scott's crotch and grinned—his teeth actually gleamed—before opening his mouth and so slowly engulfing the hard dick that the expectation of being blown became for Scott a distinctive pain worthy of de Sade.

The inside of October's mouth felt different than any he could recall—not that there were so many. Cool, slippery but dry. He could not discern the difference between the calendar boy's tongue or teeth, and had to bite his own lip to feel something normal as even the sheets beneath him seemed too smooth to grip.

The boy's gorgeous head bobbed at Scott's crotch, while soft fingers kneaded the muscles of his ass. Sweat made the freshman's skin sheen like his sudden lover's.

Scott's last breath before coming was ragged. He thrust upward, sure he would choke October, whose mouth did not budge from around Scott's dick. His orgasm had a pulse, its own heartbeat that pounded for several moments before dying. Drained, he collapsed onto the mattress.

October slid up to face him. Beads of pearly semen decorated his lips like rainwater on glass. The calendar boy bent down, eager to kiss and share the taste with Scott, who marveled at the sensations of having a mouth as smooth and cool as ice cover his own.

He missed his morning class. The romp left him so exhausted that he ignored the angry call of his alarm. He showered off all traces of October, then headed for the cafeteria. He chewed mechanically, barely recognizing what he ate. His mind remained on last night. Later, strolling on campus, lost in thought, he walked into a tree branch, scratching his face.

Explanations eluded him. Unless he considered the most far-fetched yet only acceptable answer: his uncle had sent him a magic calendar. Weird—but why not true? What a present!

Scott found it impossible to concentrate in class. He shifted in the hard seat, focused on the raging hard-on triggered by thoughts of that night. He ignored the boys he normally gawked at. He wanted only nightfall and the touch of October.

But when he returned to his dorm room, what his eager eyes sought was gone. Empty wall. He looked behind the bed in case the calendar had fallen, but found nothing but dust clumps.

That left only one answer. Scott found Grasky in the common area of the suite, slouching on the old sofa, watching ESPN while slurping down spoonful after dripping spoonful of sugar-spackled flakes.

"You wouldn't know where my calendar is?"

Grasky shrugged, never taking his eyes off the screen. "I took it down. It was creepy." An errant, soggy flake clung to his stained T-shirt.

Even though he half expected the admission, Scott was filled with anger. He could only sputter, "You had no right to do that!"

Again a shrug. He was more intent on plucking the bit of food loose and dropping it into his mouth than on arguing.

"Where is it?"

"Trashed."

Scott discovered he had little ability for considering options once panic set in. He remained relatively calm until he found the waste bin in the room empty. He turned to the suite's large rubber trash container, overflowing with two weeks' worth of dorm debris, and forced himself to thrust his hands into the garbage and root around. Only later would he realize he should have wheeled the can over to Grasky's bed and dumped the contents.

If he'd needed clumped tissues, fast-food wrappers, empty bottles of every size and shade, he'd have been in luck. What he didn't find was even a torn page, a ripped fragment of his boy-of-the-month. His fingers were sticky, the sleeves of his shirt stained.

He rushed into the hall and past the elevators, and began searching through the trash bin there. A guy leaving his room stared at him as Scott dipped deep past a battered pizza box and brushed against what he hoped were greasy leftovers and not used condoms.

Finding no trace of the calendar, he rode the elevator down to the main floor. Would he ever see October and his fifteen brothers again? *Maybe Grasky had tossed it out on his way to class.* There were dozens of trash cans around campus. As he searched one in the lobby, hot blood rushed to his face as everyone—from students walking in and out of the dorm to Mel, the old security guard who stank from pipe tobacco—gawked at him.

He admitted defeat only when Mel came over and laid a liver-spotted hand on his arm. "You're makin' quite the mess, kid." The sickly-sweet smell of cherries clung to his clothes. "If you lost somethin', best file a report in the morning." Mel nudged an apple core with his shoe and shook his head. "Make sure this lobby's clean as you found it and then you can go."

Scott made one sweep of the area immediately outside the dorm, even checking out the thick shrubbery along the building in case Grasky had tossed the calendar there. By the time he admitted defeat, the cracked glass of his watch revealed it was nearly midnight. Grime covered his hands, his arms, the front of his shirt, and his face where he had accidentally wiped sweat from his eyes.

The tightness in his chest, the sting at the corner of his vision promising that at any moment he really could just start sobbing, were not because he'd lost the best lay of his life. No, the calendar had been proof that magic existed; that reality could be bent, cheated, even seduced on occasion. His uncle's gift had made him special, different from everyone else in the world.

Scott ignored Mel's nod when he came back inside. He cursed the elevator doors when they failed to open at his command. He could feel the heat rise off his limbs as he climbed five flights.

His fingers smudged the doorknob as he returned to a dark suite. His skin cried out for a shower. But the bathroom door was shut, light inside slipping out from the cracks. He could hear the water running and more. A girl's high-pitched giggles, then moans. Andre's voice, slightly muffled.

Terrific, Scott thought, *the one time I'm filthy. And like I need a reminder Andre's hot and straight.* He came close to banging on the door, but realized that his anger was misplaced. Instead, he collapsed against the wall, partially out of sight, and waited.

He guessed ten minutes or so passed—enough time for Andre to make the girl shriek twice as he probably used up all the hot water too—before the door opened.

Wearing only a towel around his waist, Andre stepped out first. Scott found it difficult to stay miserable, if only for the moment he eyed his suitemate. Boyish and sporty came to mind. The close-cropped dark hair and long sideburns were matched by a light dusting along his chest and stomach. The light from behind caught his grin as he turned and held out a hand to the girl behind him.

If the rest of the guys he roomed with weren't so hooked on television, he might have never recognized the girl, who was also wrapped in a towel. What the hell was a celebrity doing with Andre? Not that he blamed her—but wasn't there an unwritten rule that TV stars aren't found in dorm rooms in the middle of nowhere?

The same light that revealed them both also caught Scott where he sat. He noticed that Andre had turned back, to look down at him. He felt awkward, suddenly concerned that the guy would yell at him for catching them in the midst of—well, after—a private moment.

But instead Andre greeted Scott with a chuckle, one that lasted briefly before Scott's sorry state became apparent. He then knelt down, and the towel shifted. The girl disappeared into the darker recesses of the room. "Dude, what's wrong?" Andre asked gently, as Scott stared at the tip of some *very* generous anatomy.

Drops of cool water fell from Andre's damp hair onto Scott's red face. The sensation triggered his emotions; he started rambling on about the calendar Grasky had trashed, hoping that the wet streaks on his face were more fallout from Andre's wet hair and not his own tears.

His suitemate's reaction was not what Scott expected. "You too? Shit, I thought it was just my calendar."

"What do you mean?"

Andre motioned with his head to where the half-naked celebrity had vanished. "Do you really think I could score with her?" He smirked. "I've had her…I mean, I've had her calendar for months. Nothing happened until I moved in here, then she starts visiting me at night, like she just walked off the page." He paused. "So, what, did we find the same brand or something?"

Okay, Scott thought, *all insanity aside, one magic calendar made sense—but two? Unlikely. So it had to be the suite itself.* "Not that. It's this place. Our suite, I think. It brings them to life."

"So then all you need to do is get yourself a new calendar."

Scott frowned and lightly knocked his head back against the wall. "What good will that do? Grasky will just take it down again."

"We'll worry 'bout that asshole later, okay? Take a shower. Tomorrow we'll get you a new calendar."

Enough hot water remained to wash the dirt off Scott, who could not stop thinking of Andre in the towel, or that the guy wanted to go shopping with him the next day.

In the center of the mall, not far from the food court, Scott and Andre looked over kiosks of calendars.

"What about this one?" Andre held up *Island Heat*. The Polynesian hunk on the cover with flowers in his hair looked ready to do more than hula. "I bet he'd be hot."

Scott laughed while blushing. Andre seemed more excited about buying an all-male calendar than he was.

"You keep at this and your hetero-ness will be in jeopardy."

Andre grinned. "Aww, I may be straight but I'm not narrow." He punched Scott playfully on the arm.

Scott bent down to see what was on the bottom shelf, spotting a calendar that prompted a sinister thought. He held it up to show Andre.

"You're kidding."

"Not for me. Grasky."

Andre's eyes went wide. "Damn. That would be so perfect."

Scott turned it over in his hands. *Would serve that asshole right*. "But too dangerous. I mean, what if I got in the way."

"Not a problem. You can sleep in my room tonight. Chris went home for the weekend, so the other bed is free."

"But what about you and Miss Celebrity?"

"What about it? You can watch." Andre stepped closer. "Don't tell me you wouldn't want to."

Scott stood, stunned, not sure what to say or what he even *could* say. He looked into the other boy's eyes.

"I'd want you to," Andre said in lower tone. "Would be cool. A little kinky."

Scott swallowed before nodding. "Okay." He found himself instantly growing hard at the thought of watching oh-so-hot Andre thrusting away. Scott blushed, sure that Andre knew the effect he had on him. A bit unsteadily, he took both calendars to the tired woman working the register.

When Grasky came back from dinner, he found one of the calendars hanging on the wall over his bed. "What's this?"

Scott looked up from his calculus textbook. "A peace offering."

"*Gargoyles of Notre Dame?*" Grasky lifted up the October image and glanced at the photograph underneath.

"I thought you'd like it. I have the receipt so if you'd rather have something else…"

Grasky shrugged and walked away.

Scott looked at the clock, then at the stone beast's image. Sharp teeth lined its canine snarl. He could well imagine how its bite would feel. He briefly considered tearing down the calendar, thinking that some punishments are too severe.

But then he overheard Grasky's sour voice calling someone on television a "faggot," and he remained seated. He kept one eye on the time, eager for Andre to arrive, and the other on the impending menace of the October gargoyle.

BACK AND FORWARD

Syd McGinley

'm not a foot guy, but kneeling in front of him has its own supplicant feel. He has long thin feet with a few pale golden wires on each big toe. I tug one hair with my teeth. He twitches.

"Pampering, boy, not teasing."

I tug again. "I may be on my knees but I'm not your boy," I snap.

He grins.

His extra height makes him think he's in charge no matter how often I prove he can be my bottom. It goes back and forth between us. He claims I only win when he's already wiped from rugby. He is tired today, but I've let him win. He won't be able to use that excuse again. *Lose a battle to win the war*, I remind myself. Besides, he deserves a reward today. It's positive reinforcement.

We always wrestle for who gives it up. If we stick together, I'll tell him about my college wrestling scholarship, but for now

I say: *Only Greco-Roman, Paul—not WWE flash.* I long to suplex him and watch his surprise, but I play fair. Although he's bigger and stronger, he has no technique. Good instincts, but once he's pinned or caught in a roll-up he's stuck for a counter and he'll try to cheat—fishhooking's his favorite desperation move—and I'll sneak in a move a trained wrestler would recognize. So far I've got away with it.

I squeeze his little toe hard and he opens his eyes. He's beat from his match, wrestling me, and getting his leg over. He rotates his wrist so I can see the play of first the extensors, then the flexors. Those muscles always cause the first pulse quicken, the first "I'm gonna have him" moment with any guy I fuck. And it was true with him: I saw his arm reach across for a pint, his wrist extending from a dirty rugby shirt....

I'd never knowingly met a rugby player before, but I have the French team calendar in my bedroom. I was in my "just drinking" bar and it was full of the expat Brit team who'd stopped off after an away fixture. Several sweaty obnoxious Brits were destroying my illusions by the time I saw Paul's arm stretch across the bar, and I decided to stay. It was a challenge picking up a post-match player surrounded by his mates, but if I didn't act then, I knew I'd have to find their next match. I'd feel desperate, groupie-like, and I have better things to do on Sundays than watch men thunder around in muddy herds. I like my rugby players fresh from the shower and ready to do as they're told. It was surprisingly easy to catch his eye and end up side by side in the head. We said a few inane things and Paul shook himself off more elaborately than necessary. Even for an uncut guy. He gave his foreskin a squeeze as if he were milking it, and bluntly said, "I expect service."

I laughed. "SOL, buddy. That's my line."

We paused. Ready to acknowledge and move on. But we

kept looking from each other's faces to the dicks still out in our hands.

Paul tucked himself away first. "I need someone to show me around town. I've been here months and all I know are coworkers and these rugger-buggers. I need a proper fuck like nobody's business."

"But not from me...."

He looked nervously to the stalls before he replied: "From... no..."

I paused. "I could meet you tomorrow night and show you around."

"That'd be great. Don't get me wrong—I've had a few hand jobs, but I want more. I need a dirty boy to train...." He closed his eyes. I tried not to be disappointed when his eyes opened: I wasn't who he envisioned.

"Don't we all? Well, if he's anywhere in this town he'll be at Jake's."

I never sleep with very tall men. Or blonds. Or other tops. Or uncut guys. Or even guys with tans and tattoos. I find small, dark-haired bottoms with naked, exposed cocks and milky, undecorated skin so I can see my handiwork. But we've spent months evading the fact that we prefer each other's company and bodies to those of any of the other men we've seen each other out with. We've settled into an unspoken routine: Jake's after dinner together and, more often than not, home together after a quickie with someone forgettable. We're known as "Paul-and-Dave" at Jake's. Buzzed nights on the couch turned into sleepovers in the bed and relieving each other. He claimed he was just piss proud the first time he woke up next to me with a hard-on, but he came fast enough. We're still negotiating BJs, and it took a while to get to fucking. We were both macho assholes about it, but we finally admitted it wouldn't be the first time for either of us, and taking it was all right, but not for a regular thing. Soon enough, Paul turned up with Liquid Silk and claimed he had first dibs because he brought it over. I pulled condoms from my pocket, threw them on the coffee table between us and said, "But I've already got these."

"You carry those anyway."

Two seconds later, we were rolling on the floor—him trying for a headlock and me testing if ankle locks make someone scream and tap out. I was overconfident—his weight and strength took me unawares. It'd been years since I wrestled and these days I control my boys with words or a simple pin and slap. He didn't crow about winning, but he was prompt in claiming his prize. I'd never been fucked by an uncut guy before and I watched in fascination as he prepped. The swollen red head emerged from his golden cock skin and I groaned. His dick was beautiful as the foreskin unfurled back away and then the condom parodied the moment and unrolled down over his shaft.

He grinned at me. "Position, boy."

I considered reneging. Pride—I hate being called *boy*—and desire had me locked.

Paul frowned, and suddenly I was pinned at the wrist. His large tanned hand had my right arm immobile. I felt a deep tug in my balls and I oozed precum.

"If you need to be made…," he whispered: a threat, a promise, an offer of help.

I shook my head and, hypnotized by the play of muscles under the skin of his forearms, I traced the blue of his wrist veins with my tongue and lifted my hips enough to show acquiescence. He wrenched my shorts down in one move and touched the back of my knee with a finger.

"Up!"

Magically my knees were by my ears. "Do this bit fast," I said, trying hard not to order or beg.

"You're not lubed enough...." He teased my ass with greasy fingers.

My hips betrayed me. "I mean: enter fast. I hate how the tip feels on my hole. Get your prick in so I can stop thinking about it."

He kept my ass open with his finger and held the condom tip down as he traded his finger for his cock. I've been out of practice for years, but he settled to a rhythm fast and got in deep. The stretched feeling I hate was lost in his motion. I grabbed the headboard to stop myself from putting my arms around him. I kept my eyes open. He's worth watching. A pink mottle grew under the honey-fuzz on his fifty-inch chest. His eyes were closed. They're vodka blue. Having them fixed on me as I came would've been unbearable. For a fraction of a second I slipped into being his boy, but even as my load shot I thought: *No.* Under the control of that arrogant profile and yielding to this cock all the time: *No.* He was still pounding. I was done and wanted to shove him off, but fair's fair so I lifted myself just right to trigger him. He roared as he came, and fell across me, heavy. My face was in his armpit. His fresh sweat smelled grapefruit-ginger and stung my eyes. I snorted, but he didn't move.

"Move," I said, muffled.

When he still didn't, I licked his armpit, and he reared up scowling.

"You SOB, you know I'm ticklish...."

"I didn't, but I do now."

My smirk was wiped off as he bit the inside of my knee hard while he moved to ease his cock out.

"Fuck! That hurt...."

He flicked my hip with a fingernail. "But you didn't feel

this coming out." He tossed the used rubber into the trashcan. "Figured you'd hate that too." Abashed at being considerate, he looked away. Then he sent me to the fridge for beer.

Since then we've wrestled once or twice a week. I lose enough to keep the game alive and, once I refreshed my moves, to stop him suspecting I can beat him when I want. We still go to Jake's several times a week. We part ways there for a few hours, but we always share a cab home. I never thought I'd fall for a foreigner. I'm too practical to get sucked into immigration worries or the risk of loving someone who'd have to leave, but Paul's got his green card, so it's not an issue. Assuming he wants to stay...assuming this is love we're avoiding talking about. He's dozing under my foot massage; I sneak a careful kiss on his toe. He hates open affection: it always has to be disguised.

We were at his place a few weeks ago getting ready to go out for dinner. It's an anonymous temporary apartment—he's on a yearlong contract at an engineering firm. He usually consults in the Detroit area and is used to bigger scenes than a choice between Jake's and a sports bar. He writes computer models to show just-in-time processes on plant floors. It makes me yawn. He's smart, but gets engineer-nerd-dull when he talks work. I'm not used to pretending interest: my boys listen to how my day was. He drank with his team after his afternoon match, but now he was sober and ravenous. He'd already inhaled the omelet I'd whipped up as a snack. He's always amazed I can cook without a barbeque. Another reason, he claims, he's the real top. Prick. He opens cans and eats the contents cold. Fried eggs as a Sunday treat is all he manages. Dinner was an hour away, but he had an opened can of peach halves from the fridge and was eating them dripping from the can. The juice glistened in his stubble, and some ran to his chest—he'd peeled his dirty kit off and was just in his boxers. He looked hot in the tree-filtered evening light, but

I shuddered. There's something wrong about canned peaches: so yellow, so smooth, so round, so slippery, so heavy for their volume. He hooked another out with his fingers and slid it all in his mouth, juice running down his chin. He gave a sloppy little-kid grin at my shocked face.

"Yum."

"Gross. Worse than raw eggs."

"They're good too."

"At least use a fork." I held one out to him.

He rolled his eyes but humored me. "You're so prissy, Dave. Thought you said you're a top?"

"A neat top."

He speared a peach half and held it out: "Eat!" He pushed it against my resolutely shut mouth. It smushed into my chin before I put up my hand and pulled it from the prongs.

"I hate canned peaches."

"Foodie yank…," muttered Paul, amiably enough, but I still lunged at him. He yowled as my hand drove into his shorts and smeared the still cold fruit across his balls. He grabbed my wrist and held it still. We stared for a moment then Paul cautiously put the open can down on the counter without releasing my wrist. I cupped his balls and massaged the sweet juice. I moved my fingers up and grasped his shaft. Peach spurted between my fingers as I pulled back his foreskin.

"Fuck," he whispered.

I squeezed. "Is that an invitation?"

He squirmed. "No: a request."

"No." I squeezed differently and we locked eyes again. Sometimes our dance is exquisite and sometimes it's a pissing match. That day I could tell neither of us would fold. He was tired, and I'd win easily, but then he'd bitch about it being unfair. Christ, it's complicated, and right then it was too much of price. Neither of us was in the mood to be gracious and we were both too aware of the issue that won't go away. Paul's brain was heading south. His gaze was already distant. I could have taken him. Instead I took the high road and stayed a gentleman.

"Show me how it feels too."

He took the way out I was offering and, although we each wanted to fuck the other, we ended up on the kitchen floor smearing fruit onto each other's dicks until we were a mess of drying sticky fluids. Paul held the last peach with the pit hollow nestled on my cockhead. He swirled and rotated it as he pumped my shaft. The peach flesh yielded and disintegrated as I thrust back. My head burst through the yellow flesh and, as it parted the fruit, I shot into his hand. In a second, he filled my palm with heat too. I offered him salty pulverized peach.

He frowned, all serious for a minute. "No, Dave, not even that. Nothing in my mouth."

We lay stuck together for a few minutes, neither willing to admit how good nearly being in each other's arms was.

"We should shower," he murmured. The kitchen floor was uncomfortable, and a glaze of semen and syrup stuck my thigh to the tiles. It crackled as I peeled away. He let me shower first. I wouldn't have minded showering together. I know he does it with his team. But with me it seems too intimate to him. He gave me a hard look the first time I suggested it. Shit, it's a fine line with him. *Intimate*: a bad word in his world even though he's not as badass as he thinks. Maybe a shower while we're getting hot, but an affectionate cleanup afterward? Nope.

We ran into my ex, Marky, when we were out together that night.

"Picking on someone your own size for a change, Dave?"

Paul growled at him, but Marky was unperturbed. We were

behind a table and he had the room to spin away in.

"Oh, hunting in packs is it?"

He was still sweet looking: Paul eyed him speculatively.

"Smart-mouthed," I whispered to Paul while Marky said hi to a friend.

"Jealous?"

"Me? About him?"

"Of me...."

I shook my head. "Nope, he's cute, but he'd complicate our life."

"Didn't know *we* rated a pronoun...."

Marky was smiling back at us by then. "Just warning Nino away from you, Dave."

Paul laughed aloud. "No jealousy here, huh?"

Marky's face shut down: a familiar sight. "I warn anyone I see giving Dave puppydog looks. He's not a top. He's a batterer."

The little shit was off and away from our table before I could move. "Fuck..."

Paul put his hand on my arm in case I went after Marky. "Don't give the bitch the satisfaction."

"Paul...a town this size...I'm screwed.... Marky knows everyone.... Even those who take it with a grain of salt will... shit."

"There'll be some little idiot who thinks he'll reform you."

"God, no. Besides, I never hit him like that. I hate people thinking it."

Paul's hand was still there. "Hey, Dave, I don't. And, well, there's always that pronoun...." He winked.

Fuck. I'd seen that predatory look on his face before. I didn't like being on the receiving end. I shook his hand off.

"Right, I suppose *we'll* figure something."

He took my bitterness well and laughed. "I'll bring one home for a threesome. Run the poor boy ragged keeping us satisfied."

But neither of us was happy. Paul's known as my friend, and his chances were spiraling down the crapper with mine. Neither of us wanted only one-night stands. We wanted more. And we were both mad and insulted—we treat our boys right—at least Paul said he does. He hasn't had anyone besides me since he moved here.

He's asleep now. I take the chance to look up from his feet and examine his face without being accused of mushiness. His beautiful bruise is almost gone now. He'd had a black eye from Sunday's scrum and I was shocked how fucking hot he looked. He looked dangerous. His arrogant Roman nose is made more imperious by an old break. The burst vein in his left eye wasn't pretty, but the bruise got me hard. I should have felt guilty, but, hey, I didn't hit him. He looked like a battered, victorious boxer.

I've never hit one of my boys in the face, but I've fantasized about it. My mistake was telling Marky. He freaked, and we didn't last much longer. I'd seen a photo of a bantamweight looking up into the camera from his corner stool after a lost fight. The look of meek defiance and tender violence on his face, the sweet marks on him pleaded to me: *Be mine.* I wanted Marky to look at me that way. He has a brittle beauty in his face and I imagined it, aloud, enhanced by a black eye. He'd squirmed in my embrace. Annoyed, I continued. "You have no appreciation of the aesthetics of a bruise. You'll look most elegant with a black eye. Its shades'll change so subtly. It'll give your face a perfect fragility."

Marky shook his head. He couldn't answer: shorts in his mouth and wrists tied. I was on the brink of falling for the boy so I said: "A bruised ass is a fine memory of what was done, but a bruised face will make you look so vulnerable—not like a beaten back—there I know you took a punishment. A smudged cheekbone shows you were surprised by pain. And your mouth—it'll split like a segment of orange pulled apart—the juice is so dear and pure. The tender appeal of the blood from your lip—nothing sweeter."

He'd looked scared beyond the usual delicious trepidation he showed when I reached for a riding crop, and my gut twisted. There was a timid edge to his service that evening, and I knew he'd back at Jake's soon. I used my belt hard as a farewell and a punishment for revealing a chink in my heart.

Paul had looked tough with his bruise, then, for one distracted moment, fragile and vulnerable. His face should have provoked compassion in me, but instead I got harder. I saw his distraction and flipped him. I love wrestlers in a roll up—their legs held firmly, and taut gear covering their waiting holes—the biggest of them squirm and kick and thrash and can't kip out once their knees are by their ears. Paul swore for a minute, but he's a good sport and, having conceded, he played fair. He got on all fours, and looked over his shoulder. All I could see was his black eye and Caligula nose and I nearly came against his thighs as if I were a quick-firing fourteen again. I backed off. I'd also promised myself that the next time I won I'd torture him with what he finds hardest to take: affection.

"Lie down, boy. Take it slow tonight."

He obediently slid his knees back down the bed and lay flat. He's a much better bottom than I am. Once he's lost a fight he yields into the role without my balky attitude. As soon as the scene's over, though, he'll snap back into his swagger. His muscles seemed to yearn for my touch as I rubbed his lats. He's always hot, but tonight he was hotter with his bruised face and willed obedience. Was I looking for small things that relate to my usual desire? A hint of fragility in his hard ripped body? Deep down, I knew he was the one—if we could only get this figured.

I worked down his spine—my massage almost cruel on his scrum-battered body. My thumb pressed between his cheeks and he lifted promptly. I touched his puckered hole lightly, and his hips bucked.

"Roll over...you're enjoying the mattress too much."

His cock strained into the air and there was a damp spot left on the sheet. I slapped his knees apart so I could see his hole again. Christ, I love seeing each bottom's hole for the first time: each starry ass is new—as different as snowflakes. I tickled his hole for a moment and watched him fight to stay disciplined. I teased him by rimming his belly button, its contracted puckers of skin a sealed similitude to his ass. His cock bobbed close to my face, and I held it down out of the way.

He moaned, and I got off the bed.

"Stay," I said in my dog-trainer voice. I'd pay for this next time I lost, but what the fuck. He looked disappointed as I headed to the kitchen, as if he suspected I'd stoop to ice. I rummaged in my junk drawer for a needle and grabbed rubbing alcohol from the bathroom.

He nearly broke role, but altered his tone midsentence. It came out a plea instead of a command: "Dave! No piercings..."

Surprised by the panic in his voice, I filed that tidbit away. I put my palm flat on his belly, and pushed him back down.

"Give me your left hand."

He hesitated.

I couldn't let it pass; I slapped his balls hard. "Left hand, boy."

He meekly put his wrist into my waiting grasp. I rubbed my thumb on his tendons and enjoyed the trapped fear on his face. I ran my thumb up his palm and along his ring finger, then squeezed the pad of his fingertip until it whitened. The sliver I'd noticed earlier when he tried to fishhook me was suddenly evident to him.

"My poor boy has a boo-boo...."

He snarled as I drenched his finger and the needle with alcohol, but when I wriggled the needle tip under his skin he stayed very still. I kept my face impassive, but I was elated. I'd inadvertently turned Paul into a scared little boy. The fragment came out easily, but I kept moving the needle around his fingertip. He watched closely. I traced the whorls of his fingertip with the point. His eyes unfocused and his breath slowed.

"Fingerprints, snowflakes, and assholes...all unique."

"And ears...," murmured Paul.

"Ears?" I repeated.

"Yes. INS made me show mine on my green card."

I kissed his inner wrist; he opened his eyes in shock. I smiled lazily, and then pricked his thumb deep. He yelped, and sucked the welling blood. While his thumb was still nestled on his tongue, I rammed my greased finger deep in his ass, and triggered his prostate. His untouched cock leapt and shot onto his belly. I rubbed his chest with his own cum and smeared it onto the trickle of blood on his lips. I enjoyed his refusal to lick. I knew he wanted the scene over, but I sat astride his hips and began jerking myself off.

"Tell me about your rugby team."

"What about it?"

I slapped his hip. "Tone, boy. Tell me about the game. I don't know what position you play...on the field." I leered and pumped a little harder.

"I'm a forward." He looked sullen, but his voice was neutral so I did nothing except maintain my stroke.

"What do they do?"

"We're the big guys. We get the ball from the other side, and pass it to the backs. They're meant to run it."

"Huh…," I said, and imagined Paul tackling an unlucky opponent. "So backs are the fast little ones?"

"Yeah, but a fast forward can take both positions…."

"So you switch on the field too?" Nearly too far: Paul half sat up, then flopped back. I wasn't paying attention: I was thinking about Paul tackling Marky, ramming his face into the mud. I came hard, and slid off Paul. I snapped my fingers.

"Not over yet."

He sighed, but knelt down in front of me. We end scenes with a foot rub, and Paul knows my turn isn't over until he's finished my massage, but he gets away with freely conversing as he works. He was still talking about rugby; I made myself listen. He was shocked-intrigued-worried because a gay team had joined their league, and had beaten his team. Twice. He was brooding about it. He made a snide comment about how they should have a pink kit for their away fixtures.

"You are a wanker," I said.

"Fuck off you PC yank." He gave a rueful squeeze to my toes. "I'm working on it, okay? I'm not out at home. I thought over here…but it's just as complicated…."

I flexed my big toe—he was neglecting it—and stroked his thigh with my free foot. "Limey bastard," I said affectionately.

He popped my toe. "I *am* working on it. Let me do it my way."

He's not out to his team. Two weeks ago, after they played the gay team for the first time, the winners tried to poach him after the match. Apparently, he really is a good back and forward. He finished my foot massage and sat next to me on the couch. Scene over, he cautiously revealed he was uneasy about his teammates. And guilty about the other team. He was rude to them because they asked him publicly. "Bloody nerve," he muttered. "Gay or not, you don't poach a bloke in front of his team." The return match last Sunday was how he got his black eye. He tried to avoid answering when I asked if the other team had done it deliberately, but he admitted a gay hooker had punched him in a scrum.

I smothered a laugh. I'd steered clear of jokes when I over-heard *rucks* and *hookers* being discussed, and I couldn't spoil it now. Paul's a lovely man, but hasn't much of a sense of humor. Not when he's the object anyway. I've stayed away from his matches and the drinks afterward. We've given it a try, but I don't like his friends and he hates that I won't agree to hide I'm gay. I wouldn't out him—it's his dilemma—but I won't closet myself for some hairy Brit homophobes. It pissed me off: he's scared of being seen with a gay friend. I take his point: he's in a foreign country and has few friends here, but still... I avoid him on Sunday afternoons until he's returned from hetero-land, re-adjusted his brain, come to his senses, and switched back to the man I'm starting to love. We go out to Jake's together as usual in the evenings.

He was unsettled after the first match because "his" team gave him a hard time about being cruised by fags and asked him if he was gonna switch sides.

"These are your *friends*?"

"Shit, Dave, they're just being guys. Rugby players are like that. Besides the gay team won so they're hopping mad."

But all week he had a lost, lonely look. And the next week he'd hardly talk at all about the return match. I pieced that to-gether: not only did the gay team give him a black eye, but his team cut him out of plays. We just jerked off together that night. As he slept, he moved closer. Next day, I watched him shave. I was still stretched out on the bed and I could see his reflection through the open door. Even with the remains of foam under his ears, he looked domineering and hot. He didn't know I was awake. I watched him trace the bottom rim of his bruise remnant. His shoulders sagged for a moment, and I quickly shut my eyes and faked sleep.

Looking up at his blissed-out dozing profile, I feel calm here at his feet. I can see the ghost of his bruise under his tan. I'm not kidding myself: he had to be outed by his new team and rejected by his old one before he faced reality. I'm not harsher on others than I am on myself: I took a long look in the mirror too after he'd left last week and realized if I didn't do something to keep him, I'd be left with the reputation of Dave the Abuser while he truly got poached by Simon the Hooker. I'd squashed the notion that we'd both been making do and decided taking a dive in today's wrestling match was the reinforcement he needed. I knew he was still vulnerable and I could have him for keeps if I played it right and took one for the proverbial team. He was tired but exhilarated when he came by: his new team had won. I saw him coming in my peripheral vision but I *let* him flip me. He was rough as we screwed—if he thinks I've switched because he had the balls to apologize to the scout and trade teams then he's very wrong—I get my revenge by kissing him on the mouth as he finishes. He was grumpy until halfway through the foot massage, and I worried my burst of affection/payback had ruined my plan. He's mellowed since then.

I work on his left arch a little harder so he resurfaces from sleep.

"Team invited me over for a cookout," he mumbles after a while. "You coming?"

I frown. "As your straight friend?"

He opens his eyes and glares. "As 'Paul-and-Dave.' Asshole."

"Wanker," I say fondly. I guess that makes us a couple.

DELTA BOYS

Cat Tailor

We're Delta boys, and we're totally fucked. There are only four left of our squad, and we're stuck in some godforsaken asshole of the third world. Hostile locals are coming at us with machine guns, grenades, rocks if they don't have anything else. The Delta boys are "pinned down," which is military for "can't do a fucking thing about getting out of the fuckhole where people are shooting at you."

We have about two-and-a-half walls left of the hut we're squatting in. It wasn't much of a defensible position when we ducked inside it, and it has gotten significantly worse.

Unexpectedly, there's a lull in the activity. Silence appears, for long golden moments. Brick laughs, quietly. "Fuck me, boys. Think they got tired and went home for cookies and milk?"

"Yeah, and naptime, right?" says Springer.

The nice thing about being Delta boys is that we don't have to wear those fucking drone soldier haircuts, we hardly ever wear uniforms, we don't have to run around saying "Hoo-yah" all the fucking time, and we get called out on a regular basis to go kick the living shit out of some people the good old American government can't actually admit they want the living shit kicked out of. The bad thing about being Delta boys is that when we're fucked, mostly no one knows or can do a damn thing about it.

Like now.

"Shit, boys, I don't wanna die here today. Tomorrow maybe, but not today," says Blue. He'd gotten the name from the time we were skulking around the peaceful Irish countryside, trying to be inconspicuous. Somehow the crazy fucker had managed to get a hold of some woad and had painted his entire body blue. Then he'd run yelling, naked, through the streets, with the rest of the squad trying to catch him before he woke up the nice people of Belfast. We never could get him to tell whether the naked streaking idea had occurred to him *before* he covered himself in a mild hallucinogen or *after*. Fucking crazy bastard.

I decide to give him some shit. What the fuck else were we gonna do? "What, Blue, you got some other colors you gotta paint yourself before you die?"

"I want to be there when it's pink day," says Brick, grabbing his crotch and leering. We all laugh.

"No, man, it's just, ah, fuck it. I'm gonna see if I can grab some of those fucking dead bastards' weapons. Cover me, okay?" We all laugh some more. Cover is the least possible thing in the world right now, right after chocolate ice cream and a personal visitation from the Tooth Fairy.

Springer is in charge, when we bother to acknowledge rank at all. Generally intense battle conditions prompt us to pay a tiny bit more attention to such Army crap. He tells Blue to sit his ass back down and remain in position. "And explain yourself, you dumbshit. What the fuck you gotta do?"

Blue shakes his head. We all wait. Blue isn't a guy who can stand the sound of silence. Unless he's actively sneaking up on somebody at that very second, he's running his mouth. He's fucking funny, so we don't give a shit.

He cracks. "Fine. I have a list, you know? Shit I want to do before I die or turn thirty, which ever comes first. Like every dumb fuck in the world."

I say, "What the hell could you have on it? You already jump out of airplanes and fuck hookers."

"Ha, ha, Ferret, you little weasely ass-fucker. None of your fucking business."

We wait some more.

"I want to see the world, all right? Some parts of it that aren't currently at war, you know? Some places where the U.S. of A. doesn't think of having little covert ops all the fucking time. And I want to fuck my girl outside, which somehow I never managed."

"It would help if you had a fucking girl," heckles Brick.

"Who says I don't, the way you shake your pretty ass at me all the time," shoots back Blue. This is degenerating.

Springer takes control again. "All right, you sorry fucks, if you think what Blue wants is so boring, you do better."

Brick says, "I would, but I'm speaking to an officer in the United States military, and if I admit to planning the execution of a crime, you are beholden to report it immediately."

"Oh yeah?" asks Springer. "You planning something illegal?"

"Nah. Not planning. Just if I were to have a list, and I was putting on it stuff I really wanted to do if I managed to drag my sorry ass out of this pit of hell today, I wouldn't be coloring inside the lines is all," says Brick.

"Yeah. Me neither," says Blue.

"What's all that crap about walks on the beach and the fucking fiancée then, Blue?" I ask.

"That's the shit I wrote down. You know, can't leave proof of premeditation."

A grenade bounces off the edge of a partial wall, ricocheting away from us, but not far. We hurl ourselves flat on the floor and wait to become further deafened. It doesn't explode. We sit back up.

Part of what sucks about being a third world shithole is it's hard to buy good weapons. The first and second worlds feel quite free to make a profit off your drugs, buying them with crap weapons and ammo they don't think are worth using anymore. It wasn't that bad a shot with the grenade, and might have done us some damage by knocking down the rest of that wall. If only they hadn't been shafted by the arms dealers. Again.

"What, you guys fucking serious? You got criminal plans?" I ask.

Brick doesn't take his eyes off the darkness outside the wall, but I can tell most of his attention is inside the room, focused on this conversation. "I got a lot of plans. I don't mean to die here. And if I do get the fuck out of here, well, I've been fucking trained by the Army to sneak into places I don't belong, do shit I shouldn't be doing, and get away clean. You all really think we should spend the rest of our lives being good little taxpayers?"

We think about this in silence for a while.

Springer breaks it. "I tell you what: we ain't got a fucking chance in hell of getting out of here alive." We all laugh. "But we're going to do it anyway, because we're fucking Delta boys. And if we do, we're going to carry out a solemn pact."

"What's that, boss?"

"We're each going to pick our most outrageous fantasy. Like, the one thing that might require four Delta boys to pull off, and is heinously risky and stupid, but sounds like so much fucking fun you keep thinking about it."

"The shit you just can't get out of your head," murmurs Blue.

"Exactly. Pick one thing. Keep it to yourself. Then, when we're all out of here, we'll find each other and do each guy's in turn."

"Right on, dude!" says Blue.

"Count me in," says Brick.

I know what I want. Want it so bad I can taste it. It's right there, branded across my eyeballs, taking up my whole field of vision. It can't ever happen, though. It's way too fucking wrong. But we're all going to die, right? And if God reaches down and plucks us out of this asshole of the world, well, I'll have some time to come up with another idea, right?

"Yeah, me too," I say.

Fuck.

Of course, we get out of there. When they all show up at my doorstep one fine afternoon, I pack a fucking bag and get in the fucking car.

Brick's bank robbery slides along on greased rails. It's such a smooth ride it takes all three of us to talk him out of doing it again every weekend. He's always wanted to be a gangsta.

Springer, for all his tough talk, is hiding a soft spot for his high school sweetheart. Problem is, the sweetheart has moved the fuck on and is shacked up with some dweeb who is in the country more than one weekend a month and two weeks a year. The roofies are disgustingly easy to get, and she never sees us coming. Or going. Springer hadn't ever managed to fuck her in high school, what with her virginity pact. That she tossed it out the window for this asshole a year later has been chafing his ass eternally. So he fucks her. It looks like fun, so we all fuck her. It's a good night.

Blue wants to be the first man in history to moon the president of the United States. He isn't entirely happy about our nation's foreign policy during the preceding three years, and the prankster in him just can't resist. We have endless arguments about how to get away with it, as the man has some fairly decent security. I mean, it's not like it's impenetrable, as plenty of idiot assholes have gotten a shot off at the prez from time to time. It's that the openings are unpredictable, and we don't want to get shot for this. So we rig a screen and a projector along the president's motorcade path—all checked out for bombs and such by those irrepressible Secret Police. I mean Service. Then we remotely activate a video of Blue's ass and get the fuck out of there. It's all you ever see on the news for about thirty seconds, and then the media vultures move on to the next scandal. He's happy.

Then it's my turn. I've been racking my brain trying to come up with something good to say. And then, when they all turn to stare at me, all those thoughts evaporate like fumes off a chem fire.

"Ah, forget it, guys. I don't have anything. I mean, besides like traveling and winning the lotto and shit. That's all I want. Lots of pussy and the fucking lotto. Can we do that?" I feel myself break out into a cold sweat.

Blue cocks his head, looking at me. "Boys, I think the sorry bastard's holding out on us."

"Yeah, I think so too," says Brick. "And I can't imagine why he'd want to do that, unless he was planning on turning us in or some shit."

"As your superior officer, Ferret, I suggest you open your fucking mouth and tell us what you want to do, before we have to bury you under your mama's grave to protect ourselves," says Springer.

They wouldn't do that. I think.

"No really, guys. A sea of fucking pussy, wall-to-wall women. Going from one to the other all night. And money, lots of money. Maybe we could rob another bank, and then see how many hookers we can buy in one night. Round them up from three cities or something." I'm reaching, and failing to catch.

Blue, the happy jokester, isn't smiling. He's staring me down, a cold expression I've seen on him before in battle, but never directed against one of us. "Is a Delta boy allowed to break his solemn oath to his brothers?" he asks.

"Hell no!" yells Brick.

"Roger that," says Springer. "Grab the bastard."

The three of them pounce on me. I go down fighting, but three superbly trained fighting machines outfight one superbly trained fighting machine, even on a good day. Which is not what I am having at the moment.

We are in a cheap-ass fucking motel room in Fresno, another third world asshole of strategic importance where we happen to be at the moment. I guess they don't want the manager calling the cops on us, so after they flex-cuff me they gag me. Blue grabs one of his dirty fucking socks from the pile of clothes he'd tossed off on his way into the shower earlier (mooning the president being hard work), and stuffs it in my mouth. They slap duct tape over it, and I am thoroughly fucked.

Both my wrists and my ankles are cuffed together, but I guess that isn't good enough. They yank my ankles back behind me and slap another cuff around both the others, bending me back until you can hear the "Soo-ee!" They pick me up off the floor and toss me on the bed, as if I'm not two hundred pounds of lean muscle, able to kill with my bare hands. Well, right now I'm not that, not exactly. I'm two hundred pounds of lean muscle trussed up and fucking helpless.

Better than telling them what I really want to do, though, so who the fuck's complaining?

Springer gets right up in my face. "Son, this is going to hurt me more than it hurts you." Brick sniggers. Springer hauls off and fucking punches me in the jaw. He follows it up with a quick pair of jabs to my gut, and then knees me in the nuts.

Shit. I think I black out for a second it hurts so bad. I'm pretty sure a tear or two leaks out of the corners of my eyes, involuntarily. I've been shot, twice, and that's never been as bad as the whole testicle thing. If we needed proof that God hates us, it's right there in that vulnerable sac hanging right out in the open, right in front where any-fucking-one can go shoving their jeans-clad knee into it, whenever they feel like it.

Fuck-ow.

Springer waits calmly until I stop writhing, and then says, slowly and clearly, "You make any fucking noise and I'll twist them off. Got it?"

I nod.

"You ready to talk, boy? 'Cause we can keep at this indefinitely."

I nod again. He yanks the strip of duct tape and pulls out the sock.

I decide to try begging now. "Come on, guys, don't be like this. I know I wasn't as creative as you were, but is that any reason to treat me like this? Give me a break, here. I promise, I totally swear to you on my honor as a man, that I won't ever say a word about anything we've done. Did I not point a gun at bank tellers just like you? Didn't I stick my dick in Springer's girl? Come to think of it, I bought the fucking roofies, right? Don't tell me you don't have plenty on me. Come on, let me go. That fucking hurt."

I run out of steam, and look around at three stone-cold faces. Fuck.

Springer says, "No dice, boy. We all bared our sorry little souls, and we all got what we wanted. You go hanging on to your pathetic little unrealized dream, and it's going to fester inside you. You'll get all bitter and take to drink, and then next thing you know you'll be passing marked bills and shooting your mouth off in a bar down the street from the Federal Building. You are going to talk. The only question is when."

I can't do it. I just shake my head.

Springer rolls his eyes and re-gags me. Two of them pick me up and carry me to the bathroom. They drop me in the bathtub. It's a bit of a tight fit, what with my legs up behind my back, but they shove until I'm flat on the bottom. Then they plug the drain and start filling it up with cold water. They run it until I have to lift my head to keep from drowning. They run it until I can feel the cords standing out on my neck. Then they start making runs down to the ice machine and pile buckets of ice on top of me.

Shivering makes it distinctly harder to keep one's muscles at full extension. I start getting sleepy, all the while shaking uncontrollably. My clothes are soaking wet, making me even colder. The muscles in my neck are cramping and I have to stretch them for a minute. I suck in a deep breath through my nose, hold my breath, and duck my head under the water to flex my neck the other way. Then when I have to breathe again, I heave myself back up, trying to scoot myself up the side of the tub somehow. Whenever I seem to be making any progress, Blue's hand reaches in and shoves me back down in the water.

I wonder what they'd do if I went into shock and died. Would they just leave? Or would they cook up some story about my death, refusing to leave behind a fellow soldier's body?

Is it possible this could really go that wrong? Is any of this worth the shame I'm going to feel if I just tell the truth?

I'm tired. I've stopped shivering, which frightens me. The ice is pretty much melted, but that doesn't make me any warmer. It makes me think I've been there longer than I remember, which scares me some more. I look up, and Springer is next to the tub, not Blue anymore. I meet his eyes and nod.

He doesn't quite smile, but the ice in his eyes cracks a little. He hits the drain on the tub. In moments I can set my head down, and I smile behind the tape.

Springer leans down. "Talk, and you can have hot water."

I nod. Again, the gag is removed.

Fuck it. This is just not worth dying for.

"I wanted to have sex with a guy. I never did, and I always wanted to."

There is silence in the bathroom. A long silence. Springer reaches out and turns on the water, adjusting it to warm, not hot. I'm probably hypothermic and need to be warmed slowly. He turns on the shower, aims it at my torso and legs, and pushes the other two guys out of the bathroom. They close the door.

I let my eyelids drift closed and surrender to the stabbing knives of warmth pouring over me.

Springer comes back a couple times to turn down the cold water and check on me. He doesn't speak, and I'm scared to. For a while I try to amuse myself by thinking about all the horrible things that could come out of my little disclosure, ranging from dishonorable discharge to my father's death by a heart attack. Eventually I figure out this isn't very amusing, and just sorta go numb.

Until the door opens again, and Springer is standing there, naked but for dog tags and combat boots, holding a bottle of JD by the neck. "On your feet, soldier!" he barks. I'm too surprised to laugh. "A deal's a deal, and we're your squad."

Grinning widely, he reaches down and grabs me under my arms, hauling me out of the tub like I weigh nothing. Maybe I don't to him, as he's six-four and built like an APC, thick veins standing out on his forearms even at rest. I'm not small, but I'm pretty sure his neck is as big around as my thigh.

He kicks out a foot behind him to shut off the shower and drags me dripping into the room. I'm dropped on the floor, totally stunned. Looking up, I can see three Delta boys, all wearing Springer's new fashion choice. They burst out laughing at the look on my face, and Brick and Blue clink their beers together.

"I think the poor bastard's going to die of a heart attack," says Blue.

"Yeah," agrees Brick, "He makes it through Delta training, when nine outa ten guys wash out, and dies a sudden death 'cause he's embarrassed about being a fucking pervert. We're gonna put that on his tombstone."

Another clink, another swallow of beer. "Glad you're enjoying yourselves," I finally manage to say. "Want to clue me in on what the fuck you're all doing?"

"Hangin'," says Blue, with what I would have to swear is a giggle if he weren't a knife-eyed practical-joking killing machine.

Springer takes a seat on the edge of the bed. He reaches out to kick my legs until I'm facing him. Then he puts his boots up on my hip, like I'm a trussed-up fucking footstool. "Here's the deal, Ferret. We had us a little debate. First we thought about picking up a trick, you know, cruising the alleys downtown for a fourteen-year-old piece of willing ass. Plenty of 'em ready to do whatever you want for a place to stay for the night and some food, much less actual cash, for which they'll start volunteering to do shit you didn't even think to want until they brought it up."

He leans back a little, dropping his hand to casually adjust the position of his dick on his thigh. If I could shake the feeling of having dropped into another fucking dimension, I might think it's growing a little bit.

"But we ruled that out."

Brick scowls. "Yeah, little fucking shit could figure out there was an opportunity to make some money, being able to finger four big ole soldier types as faggots. No fucking way am I losing my benefits over your getting a chance at a gaping faggot asshole."

"And if we didn't want to get fingered, we'd have to kill the little fucker, and we all thought that murder, while appropriate in certain circumstances, was probably an extreme measure for your chance at that flapping orifice," says Blue.

"Ha! Yeah. Exactly," says Springer. "So then what? We thought about getting creative, you know, advertising for a bottom to get fucked up the ass blindfolded by a well-hung military type, on the S/M personal ads or some shit. But, we ruled that out for two reasons. One, you said 'have sex with,' which is not the same thing as 'fuck a pervert up the ass while he doesn't know it's me.' Thank God you didn't say 'make love to,' because we didn't know how on earth we'd work out a faggot being in love with you without knowing it was you. Anyway, it seemed fraught with the potential for fuckups, and weird on top of it."

"You ever going to come to some kind of point?" I ask. "You hire strippers instead?" I'm starting to hope, and the feeling is making me queasy inside. It's not like I ever think about the guys in a, you know, sexual way. But if they're going to stand around naked and talk about me having sex with other guys, well, I'm starting to shift my perspective. Brick has this soft blond hair that I can now see is a fine down over his entire body, with a thick piece of meat hanging in the middle of a nest of it. He looks like every girl's surfer-boy fantasy.

Springer's cock is definitely growing, and now he drops a hand down to stroke it absently, like he doesn't even realize he's doing it. Coy fucker. "No, Ferret. No strippers. Just us. Like we said, a deal's a deal. We're the ones with the motivation to keep quiet about it. You're the one who clearly needs a little more bonding with the guys."

Brick has moved around, and is standing behind me. He leans down to talk right into my ear, low and mean, and I jump. "We were going to draw straws for who had to do it with you. But the boss overruled us, saying that'd give two guys a hold over the other two. So instead, we drew straws for who has to take it up the ass."

I feel a wave of heat travel from my cock up to my face in one long flush. Holy shit. Were they fucking serious?

"Are you fucking serious? Don't jerk me around, you sorry bastards."

Blue says, "We're not jerking you around. We're all going to have sex with you. Once you tell us which one of us you hope got the short straw."

I'm lightheaded, and so I say the first thing that pops into my mind. "Turn around and let me see what you got, and then I'll make up my mind."

Laughing, the three of them line up in front of the bed, wagging their asses at me. "Brick, definitely. That blond surfer-boy fuzz. That's what I'd like to be slamming home inside of."

"Fucking pervert," says Brick.

"Too bad," says Springer. "You got me instead."

"Shit, man, how the fuck am I supposed to get anything wedged inside that rock you call a butt?"

"I don't know, but you better figure it out. This ain't gonna happen again," says Springer.

I'm starting to shiver again. "Am I going to have to enjoy this experience sopping wet and hog-tied?"

"Nah. We'll rescue you." Blue laughs, whipping out his steel eight inches. Springer pulls his legs back out of the way. Blue slides the knife under the flex cuff around my ankles, freeing them with a slight twist. He cuts the laces on my boots and strips them off me, straightening out my legs in the process. Thank fucking God. Then he slides the point of the knife under the cuff of my pants, and rides it all the way up my thighs. The wet fabric falls apart like your sister's legs. It only takes him a few seconds to rid me of all my clothing, until I'm wearing nothing but wrist cuffs and dog tags.

"Want to release the wrists, guys? These things fucking suck, you know."

Springer reaches a hand down to grab my hair. He pulls hard, and I scramble to get my legs under me. In one smooth motion, he gets me up from the floor onto my knees, and shoves my face into his crotch.

Oh, fuck.

Goddamn.

Halle-fucking-lujah Jesus.

I don't hesitate. I just open wide and suck him into my mouth. Oh, shit, he feels good. It's unbelievably soft, as soft as pussy even. It tastes like, oh, I don't know. Like a man. Like good clean man, the same smell that gets so intense in cramped quarters when we haven't bathed for a week, but fresh and good. It's like sex, only a side of sex I never thought I'd get to taste.

Then I stop thinking, as he's getting bigger in my mouth. Working my tongue around him, I quickly fall into a rhythm I hope he likes. I'm trying to do what chicks have done to me, when it's been good. God, it's getting huge. I can't fit all of him

in my mouth anymore, and I'm starting to feel like one of those
ineffectual bitches who piss me off when they're giving me head,
dancing around on the tip of it.

Apparently Springer feels the same way about this technique.
He clamps his hand on the back of my head and slams me forward until he's lodged in my throat. It's a frightening feeling,
choking on cock, but I think to try swallowing, and the pressure
eases. "Yeah, that's it, you little faggot bastard. Swallow."

Brick and Blue think this is hysterical. I start to wonder if
I'm ever going to breathe again. But oh, the feeling of having my
face pressed against the scratchy hair of his belly, of knowing
there's nuts under my chin and a stubbly-faced man above.

Springer relaxes his hold on my head, and I pull back. He
growls, but stops when I slam back down. I'm trying to show
him I'm not working to get away; I don't care if I breathe. I'm
just trying to make it good, to fuck him with my throat, to swallow him over and over as if I'll never eat food again.

His hand is riding on the back of my head, then dropping
down to grab hold of the back of my neck. He clamps on, gripping me, and starts shoving me a little faster. I get the point and
speed up, but he doesn't stop pushing. It's violent, nasty, this
hard push every time I suck all of him inside my bruised throat.

I'm hard as marble.

Springer grunts, and his hips move in time. Soon, it's going to
be soon. I speed up still more, working as hard as I can between
the pushing hips and the gripping hand. Then he bellows and
holds me against him. I can't breathe, and his spunk is shooting
into me in thick globs I can feel hitting the walls of my throat. I
suck harder, wrapping my tongue around him, and swallow it
all down.

"Me next," says Brick, and I feel myself come. Just like that,
hearing that deep, mean voice tell me what's coming, and I'm

shooting all over the bedspread and the floor.

"Hey boys, I think he likes me," says Brick.

"Nah, that's 'cause he had such a good time sucking down this wand of luuuv," says Springer.

Springer releases me, and I pull back just enough to breathe. I hold him in my mouth, gently, careful not to be annoying in the after-come sensitive zone. Springer hits me in the forehead, knocking me off him. "Fucking faggot," he says, with a smile on his face. Then he flops back down on the bed and pretends to snore.

Brick snaps his fingers, and I shuffle over to him on my knees. He's standing three feet away, and could easily have walked over to me, but he makes me get the rug burn instead. He's already hard. I look up at him, smirking, and say, "I guess Springer isn't the only one who enjoyed that, eh Brick?"

He backhands me, grabs my hair, and shoves me onto his cock. Oh man, a guy could get used to this. Just when I'm establishing a good pace, getting the hang of swallowing this thicker piece of meat, Brick pushes me off him. Blue slides a knife through my wrist cuffs, and picks me up to throw me on the empty bed. Brick lies down on one side of the bed, and I kneel over him, on all fours, getting right back to work.

I feel a warmth hitting my asshole. It's smooth, and thick. I can see just enough behind me while staying on Brick's cock to tell it's Blue back there, but I can't see what he's doing. Whatever it is, he's working something inside me with his fingers, I'm pretty sure.

Then I feel another kind of pressure, a thicker pressure, and a thrill runs through me, like a shaft of electricity through my dick. It turns me on so much my nuts are pulling up against my dick already, and I just came minutes before. Blue is pushing his cock up my ass, shoving himself inside me while I suck on Brick.

It hurts, and I try to relax. Relaxing is key, right? For a minute it feels like he's going to shove my asshole right up inside me, and then I give way. It opens up like it's always known how, and Blue slides home.

There's a burning, and an intense feeling that I need to take a shit, and I'm so overwhelmed I can hardly keep from biting Brick's dick off in my distraction. I'm full where I've never been full. I can feel Blue's nuts, fuzzy against my ass. I feel myself wriggling my hips in my delight, not quite pushing back onto him, but twisting around a bit.

Then he begins to slide back out. At first I panic, thinking he's going to stop. Then he clamps his hands on my hips, and I realize he's going to start fucking me now. Oh, shit. Am I ready? It still burns, still feels hugely opened where nothing has ever been opened before.

Ready or not, he starts coming back in. He goes slowly at first, like a buddy would, and then speeds up. Pretty soon I'm working on and off Brick in time to the slamming I'm taking behind. Blue's thrusts drive me further against Brick's belly, grinding my nose into his pubic hair. Whatever he shoved up my ass is amazing. It's staying slick and smooth, no matter how long he pounds away at me. Sometimes he gives a little twist when he's all the way home, and I swear I can feel every fucking pubic hair as it slides across the sensitive skin of my asshole.

Springer joins us on the bed, lounging across the bottom of it, watching us. He's stroking his cock again, and it's already half-hard. Hoo-yah. From what I can see out of my peripheral vision, he's studying my face.

"Boys, I think this asshole's going to shoot another load," says Springer. "Can't have that, can we?"

"Sir, no, sir!" barks Blue, giving extra emphasis to his thrust. I pull my head off of Brick's cock enough to say, "Why the fuck not?" and then Brick shoves me back down onto him, keeping his hand on my head now.

"Well, your asshole will tighten up, for one thing. And we all have plans for it. But you'd get fucked either way, enjoying it or not. Really, it's because I feel like being a mean son of a bitch, and you can't stop me."

I can't? Watch me come, you sadistic motherfucker.

Springer must have read this sentiment in my expression, what of it he can see around my distended cheeks. He reaches out and snaps my dick with a rubber band. Hard.

Fuck-ow. God-fucking-damnit. I feel my hard-on drop two inches in dismay. That fucking hurt.

It's made all the other sensations more clear, though. I can feel every ridge of Blue's tremendous cock up inside my asshole. I can feel Brick getting close to coming, hear the slight changes in his breathing. It makes me hungry, makes me want to get him off, so I can suck that pleasure out of him.

I speed up and turn myself into a regular fucking Hoover, giving it everything I have. Brick thrusts home in my throat, slamming so hard I wonder if he's going to come out the other side. He starts shooting, and I know my dick has recovered from Springer's blow.

So of course he does it again. Fucker.

Instead of swallowing right away, I let some of Brick's splooge run back out of my mouth. It makes a puddle in the hair at the base of his dick, and I suck it out, licking it up. I have to chase a little down onto his balls, and he seems to like this. I do too. I spend a little while there, sucking first one and then the other inside my mouth to roll them around, finally figuring out I can fit them both inside if I'm careful, all while Blue's pulverizing my anal cavity in the most amazing way. I thought I'd learned to like pain in Basic. This was awesome.

I could feel my dick twitching at the thought, and then there it was, that fucking rubber band again. I turned my head to look at Springer. "Hey, you lousy rotten fuckhole. You going to keep doing that all night?"

Just then Blue hollers out, pushing me forward so hard I'm flattened onto the bed and pushing Brick onto the floor. I can feel the pulses of his come hitting inside me, and his dick is twitching like a dying fish. In a good way, you know? My head is still turned toward Springer, and he grins slowly and rolls over, showing me his ass.

"No, not all night," he says.

Fuck yeah. Oh, I can't wait to find out what this feels like. I've boned a couple chicks up the ass, sure. But never one with an ass as rock hard as Springer's, and most definitely never my C.O. Now I remember why he was making me keep my dick hard. Short straw.

I push Blue off of me without so much as a backward glance, done with that and on to the next. Growling deep in my throat like half the zoo gone mad, I crawl across the bed to Springer. I reach out my hand, and there's Blue, shoving a big glop of Crisco in it. Ah, it all comes clear now. Yeah, that would do it, wouldn't it? And really, who needs a condom among buddies?

I want to do this standing up, with some real leverage. I launch myself over Springer and to the floor and pull his legs off the bed with my empty hand. I kick his feet apart to give myself some room, and smack the handful of grease into his crack. He laughs like he doesn't care about what's about to happen to him, and I'm filled with nothing but the desire to make him stop thinking it's so fucking funny.

I use what's left on my hand to grease up my dick, because I don't have any patience for working it up inside him. What goes in with me is all he's gonna get. I look down at myself, and I'm pleased with what I see. I'm just as big as the rest of the boys, with a wicked curve none of them have. The ladies like it on their G-spots. Wonder if Springer's prostate is in for a fucking treat?

"Hold still, you fucking bastard. I'll show you what faggot ass is all about," I say, putting one hand on his throat and the other on his hip. I want to choke him a little as I fuck him, so I get my handhold ready. I use my dick to push his asscheeks apart, and realize I can't see where I'm going. Fucker's holding his cheeks together.

Dropping him, I put both hands on his ass, spreading his crack. I line up my dick and press, pushing at his tight hole. It's an innocent little pink pucker like anyone's, with a ring of brown hair pointing at the target. The target doesn't give way. The target fights back, like my dick isn't made of steel at this point.

Titanium asshole trumps steel dick. I laugh out loud at this stupid thought. Then I reach around and grab his nuts. Giving them a hard twist, I growl in his ear, "Let me in, you rotten piece of shit, or I'll take them off."

One more push, and the gates of heaven open wide. "Fucking thank you very much," I say.

Oh, I mean it. Sliding in, it's better than any of the rest of it. It's tight, and hot, and I know it hurts him on so many levels. It's just wrong, plain wrong, and I have to fight hard not to come right then. No, I want to make this last.

I move slowly until I'm all the way up against him. I let go of his nuts, and move my hand up to his dick. "See, I can be reasonable," I say in his ear. For a while I'm jacking him off while fucking his ass, and then I lose track of him. Fuck him, let him rub himself on the bedspread if he wants to get off.

I slap my hand back around his throat, and then add the other one. Lacing my fingers together, I pull his upper body off the bed, up against me. I'm pulling him back onto my cock with my hands around his throat, and his asshole tightens up. Fear? Whatever the reason, it feels fucking good. I'm slapping up against his ass so fast there're wet smacking sounds with every thrust. His sphincter must be on fire, but it's the best thing I've ever felt. Fuck him.

Movement on the other bed catches my eye, and I see that Brick and Blue have found a way to ease the boredom. Brick's pounding away in Blue's ass as hard as Blue pounded mine. Yeah. I watch them, timing my thrusts to match theirs. Pretty soon I'm grunting in time with Brick, getting louder and louder, and then I come so hard I lose myself entirely, blasting right out of my body somewhere, somewhere nice.

When I come back to myself, Springer is peeling my fingers off his throat, coughing like he's been choked. Oops. It takes me a minute to get enough neurons firing to send a message to my hands, but when I do I let go. He seems grateful.

I'm still inside his asshole, and I rub myself up against his hard ass one more time before pulling out, dripping come off my dick onto the floor. Fuck the carpets. They were a Luminol nightmare before we checked in, that's for fucking sure.

I guess Brick came too, because he and Blue are lying on the bed, smiles on their faces. Fuck yeah.

"Let's go rob another bank and come back here and do it again," says Brick.

"Fuck the bank," says Springer. "Let's go get all-you-can-eat oysters and come back here and do it again."

Blue grins, slow and wide. "It ain't over until we say it is."

"Hoo-yah," I say. "Cheaper than hookers."

"Safer than roofies," says Springer.

"Ah well," says Brick. "Fuck the banks."

We all cheer.

RING TONES

C. B. Potts

My phone rings at a particularly annoying pitch, shrilly demanding that I stop whatever I'm doing and answer it. It's impossible to ignore the sound it makes—a high-pitched squeal somewhere between nails down a chalkboard and the yelp a puppy makes when you step on its tail.

Marco set it that way intentionally.

"I've got to get you to pick up the line somehow, don't I?" he'd asked, when I protested the god-awful noise coming from the phone. "Otherwise, you'll just let the machine pick up."

"That's why I have a machine. So it can answer the phone when I'm busy."

"But Gregory, you're always busy." Marco pouted, his lower lip plumping out in a most seductive manner. "Too busy for me."

Pavlovian, I reach for him, chewing my way down the taut expanse of his neck before guiding him to my bedroom. "I am never too busy for you."

But in truth, sometimes I *am* too busy for him. When I'm working in my studio, totally immersed in a project, my mind is occupied by the heavy metal I sculpt. I'm thinking about torches and
structural integrity, safety and artistry—not to mention trying to
capture a fleeting vision for all time.

I think Marco understands this. He's an artist too—albeit a
digital graphic artist, whatever the hell that means—and he tries
not to call when he knows I'll be in the studio.

But there are other times that perhaps he would not understand.

Like this morning. I'd called one of the boys from the bar,
one of the young ones who understand that perhaps I do not
always want to be Daddy. Perhaps I do not always want to be
on top, getting my cock sucked and plunging into widely spread
cheeks. Sometimes it is better to please than to be pleased, and
this one understands that. I know his name, but we don't use it.
I just call him *Sir*.

"Gigi," he tells me—and he calls me Gigi to keep me in my place,
to remind me that he is the manly one in this encounter—"get
down on your knees."

And so I do, the joints creaking as much from lack of practice
as age. I'm only fifty-two, after all.

"Hands behind your back, Gigi." The silk scarf he loops
round my wrists is more symbolic than practical, but that
doesn't matter. What matters is that I'm ceding control to him,
making myself helpless before the power of his desire.

Although the knots hold firm when I try them. That alone
sends the blood pumping into my cock, my erection jutting
straight out.

Sir notices and laughs. "What a dirty girl you are," he says,
rubbing his jeans-clad calf along the length of my manhood.

"But we're not here for your pleasure, are we? We're here for mine."

He reaches for his waistband—one of the things I love about these encounters is that he stays almost entirely dressed throughout, while I'm naked on the floor—and then takes his fingers away.

"Ask for it, Gigi."

"Please, Sir, let me suck on you. Put your dick in my mouth, please." I grovel, begging him for the chance just to lick the sweat from his balls.

My cock is almost slapping against my stomach.

He lets me plead some more and then unzips his fly. There's no underwear to contend with—he knew why he was coming over, after all. His cock springs out, long and thick, with a blunt, broad head and a fringe of black pubic hair curling around the base.

I moan, trapped somewhere between anticipation and need.

He smiles and touches his shaft, running his long, tapered fingers over the length of it. "I do have a nice prick, don't I?"

It's not a rhetorical question, and I hurry to assure him that he is in possession of the most wondrous, desirable, gorgeous piece of manflesh I've ever seen.

"Well, Gigi, since you like it so much, I'll let you have a taste." He twines his fingers in my hair, using my gray locks to guide my watering mouth to his shaft.

His grip is firm, and for the first few seconds, all I can do is slobber over his cockhead, swiping my tongue across the velvety, hard surface. He likes it when I point my tongue for a dip into his piss-slit, so I do this repeatedly, delighting in his throaty moans.

He rewards me by feeding more of his meat into my mouth, pushing past my lips in a quest for my tonsils. My tongue traces the network of veins scrolling around his shaft, and my cheeks ache from stretching to contain his girth.

I slide my head back and forth as much as his grip will allow. My spit coats his shaft, and it emerges shiny and slick from my mouth, only to plunge back in, deeper with every stroke.

He increases the pace, thrusting his hips against my face until the broad tip of his cockhead bumps against the back of my throat. All my years of cocksucking, and I still haven't been able to master that involuntary gag reflex.

"Let me fuck your throat, Gigi," Sir pants, drawing my head back a fraction. "I want to come in your stomach." I tip my head back just a fraction, the signal we've developed to let him know he's free to barrel on full bore.

And barrel on he does, slamming into my mouth as fast as he can, short rabbit strokes pushing his cock into the very top of my throat, shifting my tonsils out of position with the force of his urgency.

His pubic hair is scratching against my face, my nose crashing into his stomach with every stroke. My mind is reeling from the lack of oxygen, every breath I take full of nothing but his scent, his sweat, his passion.

When he comes, he erupts with a hot load that spills down my throat faster than I can swallow. It bubbles past my lips, dripping onto my chest.

Sir pulls out of my sloppy mouth, wiping his soft shaft against my hair before tucking himself back into his jeans and zipping up. He gazes at me, spunk-covered and rock hard, kneeling naked on the floor before him.

"You're a mess, Gigi. A girl should take a little more pride in her appearance." None too gently, he tips me forward so I fall onto my stomach. I feel my erection pinned between my weight and the unyielding floor.

"Nonetheless, I think you deserve a little reward for such a spectacular blow job." He walks to the corner of the room and rummages in his duffel bag. "Don't you?"

"Please, Sir, I'd much rather you fucked me," I beg, desperate to feel his cock inside me.

"Oh, I will, don't you worry," he replies. "But first I want to see if this works." He kicks my legs apart and squats next to my ass. "Do I need to lube you up or are you ready for me?"

A thick finger thrust past my sphincter answers his question. "You're shameless. What are you going to do if that boy of yours wants to rim you and finds you taste of cherry lube?" He begins to pump his finger in and out rhythmically, and soon my hips rise to meet his thrust. "Or are you such a desperate slut that you just don't care?"

"As long as you keep doing that, I don't care about anything at all," I reply. "Give me another finger?"

"I've got something better than that," he says. I feel a cold, thin shaft slipping between my cheeks. "A silver bullet, as it were."

Suddenly I am stuffed full. The cool metal pushes in just far enough to rest against my prostate.

My breath is coming quick and shallow, and I thrust my hips upward, desperate for Sir to give me more.

"See, that is nice," he says. "You're already squirming like a fish on the line. And it's got a little handle so I can fuck you with it." He slides the dildo back and forth, sending paroxysms of pleasure shooting through my body. "Plus there's an added surprise."

Just then my phone rings, its caterwauling cries cutting right through my moans.

"What the hell is that?"

"It's my phone," I gasp, panting as he continues to plumb my bowels.

"Should *I* answer it?" He twists the shaft within me, stimulating a whole new set of nerves. "Or do you want to talk?"

"The...machine...will...get...," I pant, my cock flexing madly beneath me.

"But that ringing is getting on my nerves," Sir says, straightening up. "I think I will get it." He reaches down and flips a switch on the dildo before striding over to the phone.

I didn't know if he answered it or the machine picked up or what—and I didn't care. When Sir flipped that switch, he set the dildo to vibrating what felt like a million times a second. And it was still nestled right against my prostate.

Naked, bound, on the floor of my own apartment, I shot my load while a buzzing metal shaft shook between my cheeks. All the while Sir looked on, a superior smile on his face.

Would I have come without him watching? Probably, but not as hard. And he knew it.

"You do enjoy making a spectacle of yourself don't you?" he asked, plucking the toy from my bowels and tossing it into his bag. I blushed scarlet, feeling the red heat of embarrassment all the way down to my shoulders. "But I must admit the sight was rather stirring. Makes me want to fuck you."

He knelt between my legs, and slipped his cock into my well-stretched bung. "But don't worry, Gigi. I muted your phone, so we won't have to worry about any more interruptions."

Once he had the initial orgasm out of the way, Sir could fuck for hours, and we enjoyed a long, leisurely screw. Or he enjoyed it, while I, lying in the slick puddle of my own pleasure, moaned through the ecstasy of being thoroughly used.

He untied me and left. A quick shower and much-needed mop-up of my study later, I was revitalized.

A blissful afternoon in the studio followed, where I did some of the best work I've managed in a long time. Completely wrapped up in questions of form and line, I didn't notice time passing. The sun had dropped well below the horizon when Marco burst into my studio, looking frantic.

"Gregory! What's wrong? Why didn't you answer the phone?" He glanced around the studio, looking for bandages, perhaps, or iodine solution. "I thought you were hurt in here!"

"Marco," I soothed, suppressing the urge to shoot a guilty look at the phone. "I just never even heard it ring. I'm sorry. Of course I would have answered you. I've been right here the whole time." The words were easier to say, of course, because they were all true, if one discounted that first call.

"There must be something wrong with your phone." Marco stalked out into the hallway to retrieve my mobile. "You've got this on *mute*!"

"Do I?" I walked out to join him. "I dropped it earlier. Maybe I hit a button? Is it broken?"

"No," he laughed. "You just slide this little lever here on the side. It's not broken." He kissed me on the nose, beaming with affection. "My poor Daddy. You really are helpless with this stuff, aren't you?"

"Absolutely," I replied. "Whatever would I do without you?"

ABOUT THE AUTHORS

NICK ALEXANDER was born in 1964 in the United Kingdom and has lived and worked both there and in the United States, and has traveled widely. He now lives with two cats and three goldfish in Nice, France. He is editor of the biweekly satirical news site www.BIGfib.com, and his work has appeared in the UK magazine *reFRESH*. His successful first novel, *50 Reasons to Say Goodbye*, was published in 2004 to much critical acclaim. *AXM* magazine described *50 Reasons* as "Gay literature at its finest and most original." The sequel, *Sottopassaggio*, was published in 2005 to positive reviews. For more information or to contact the author please visit his website at www.nickalexander.com.

JONATHAN ASCHE's work has appeared in numerous magazines, including *Playguy*, *Inches*, *Torso*, *Honcho*, *Men*, and *In Touch for Men*, as well as the anthologies *Friction 3*, *Three the*

Hard Way, Manhandled, Buttmen 2 and *3, Best Gay Erotica 2004,* and *Best Gay Erotica 2005.* He is also the author of the erotic novel *Mindjacker,* published in 2003. He lives in Atlanta with his husband, Tomé.

One Halloween, **STEVE BERMAN** gave head to a straight guy in a graveyard. Lately he hasn't matched the audacity of that October act with anything other than writing stories with queer and weird elements. He has three times been nominated for a Spectrum Award, has published more than sixty short stories and articles, and has a collection of odd plush monsters. His young adult novel, *Vintage,* featuring a very gay ghost, releases in 2007. He currently resides in southern New Jersey, which is the only state that has an official devil.

An advocate for the fluid nature of boundaries in art+word+ deed, **JOE BIRDSONG** and his work have been featured in *Gay City News,* the *Village Voice, HX, Next,* www.nyhotsex.com, *Creative Loafing, Popcorn Magazine,* and the *Southern Voice.* He is a board member on *the* online forum in NYC, www.motherboardsnyc.com. When not writing, constructing an erotic art film (*The PunkSpunk Series*), or curating flaming forums [*Flaming Slips (of the Tongue), Qwe're Musicfest*], Birdsong receives mail for Quentin Crisp at his East Village home.

KAL COBALT shares an apartment with a number of lively muses, an array of technogeek paraphernalia, and as steady a supply of green tea ice cream as possible. Just four blocks away, there is a tree-laden, perfectly paved neighborhood awaiting Sunday afternoons. K. C.'s stories have seen print online in *Velvet Mafia, Clean Sheets, Fishnet, hand.tooth.nail,* and *Suspect*

Thoughts, and in *SMUT Magazine* and others. Find out more at www.kalcobalt.com.

JAIME CORTEZ is a cultural worker in California. His writing has appeared in a dozen anthologies, his visual art has been exhibited at numerous California galleries, and he edited the anthology *Virgins, Guerrillas & Locas.* He has worked as a high school teacher in Japan, at the AIDS Memorial Quilt, and at Galería De La Raza, and has lectured on art and activism at Stanford, Berkeley, UC Santa Barbara, University of Pennsylvania, and the Yerba Buena Center for the Arts. He is pursuing his MFA in art at Berkeley, and can be reached at beardevil@hotmail.com.

WAYNE COURTOIS is author of *My Name Is Rand.* His work has appeared online in *Suspect Thoughts* and *Velvet Mafia,* and in journals and anthologies such as *Harrington Gay Men's Literary Quarterly; Of the Flesh; Love Under Foot; Best Gay Erotica 2005; Out of Control; Walking Higher: Gay Men Write About the Deaths of Their Mothers;* and *I Do/I Don't: Queers on Marriage.* He lives in Kansas City, Missouri. Visit him at www.waynecourtois.com.

DOUG HARRISON has written book reviews, essays, and short stories for the 'zines *Black Sheets* and *Body Play.* His short stories have appeared in the anthologies *Men Seeking Men, Still Doing It, Best Bisexual Erotica, Best Gay Erotica 2001, Best S/M Erotica, Tough Guys, Guilty Pleasures, Kink, Bearotica, Sex Buddies,* and *Bad Boys.* He is working on a novel about the late-twentieth-century leather scene, and lives in Hawaii with his partner Bill Brent, and can be reached at pumadoug@hawaii.rr.com.

VINCENT KOVAR writes articles, essays, fiction, and plays. His fiction has appeared in *Blithe House Quarterly*; his non-fiction has been published in *Hungry? Seattle* and *Seattle: 150 Years of History*, as well as in a variety of venues, including PlanetOut.com, *Unzipped Monthly*, *Pride Magazine*, *Watermark*, *Southern Voice*, *Texas Triangle*, and *Seattle Gay News*. He lives in Seattle.

DAVID MAY first made his mark writing for *Drummer* and other gay skin magazines in the 1980s, and is the author of *Madrugada: A Cycle of Erotic Fictions*. His work has appeared in numerous magazines and anthologies, including *Mentsch*, *Kosher Meat*, *Flesh and the Word 3*, and *Best of Best Gay Erotica 2*. He lives in Seattle (where he is still working on that damn novel) with his husband and two cats.

SYD MCGINLEY has lived in the United States since 1989; teaches college in a red state; thinks students would do better if they'd just do as they're told, damn it; stays sane writing dirty stories; wrestles with the obligatory novel; and under-appreciates beloved Joe far too often. Publications for 2006 include *Mimosa* from Torquere Press's Cherry Bomb line.

SEAN MERIWETHER's fiction has been defined as dark realism. His work has appeared in *Best Gay Love Stories 2006*, *Skin & Ink,* and *Best of Best Gay Erotica 2*. In addition to writing, he has the pleasure of editing two online magazines, *Outsider Ink* (www.outsiderink.com) and *Velvet Mafia: Dangerous Queer Fiction* (www.velvetmafia.com*).* Sean lives in New York with his partner, photographer Jack Slomovits, and their two dogs. If you are interested in reading more of his work, stalk him online at www.seanmeriwether.com.

SCOTT POMFRET is coauthor of *Hot Sauce*, the first-ever same-sex marriage novel. *Hot Sauce* is one of the Romentics-brand romance novels for gay men (www.romentics.com). He also writes short stories that have been published in *Post Road*; *Genre*; *Fresh Men: New Gay Voices*; *Best Gay Love Stories 2005* and *2006*; *Best Gay Erotica 2005*; and many other magazines and anthologies. For more information, visit www.scottpomfret.com.

C. B. POTTS, dedicated to providing the best one-handed reading available, churns out tons of smut from her Adirondack Mountain home, in between bouts of science fiction and responsible journalism. More info at www.cbpotts.net.

RICHARD REITSMA grew up in the Great Lakes State, and now teaches Spanish and Comparative Literature at Goucher College in Baltimore, specializing in contemporary literary movements, literature of the Americas, magic realism, and gay and lesbian studies. He is working on his PhD through Washington University–Saint Louis, examining the construction of sexuality in plantation fiction from the American South and the Caribbean; and he has published an interview with author Christopher Bram in *Harrington Gay Men's Quarterly*. He is currently working on a collection of short stories. "Argentina" was previously presented at the Lynchburg College Gender Studies Symposium in 2001.

ROB STEPHENSON's writing appears online and in print in such publications as *Mascara*, *Skin & Ink*, *Between the Palms*, *Blithe House Quarterly*, *BUTT*, *Dangerous Families*, *Problem Child*, *Best Gay Erotica*, *Tough Guys*, and *Perspectives on Evil and Human Wickedness*. He has written introductions to two of Samuel R. Delany's books, *HOGG* (Fiction Collective 2), and *The Motion of Light in Water* (a Triangle Classic from Insight-Out book club). Visit www.RAWBE.com

CAT TAILOR's work includes the BDSM novel *In the Spider's Web*, the adult game *The Pansexual Perverts' Play Pack*, the sex advice column "Chasing Your Tail? Ask Cat: Advice for Fuckers, Players, and Perverts" on www.shadesbeyondgray.com, and short stories that have appeared at www.twobigmeanies.com, www.sexuality.org, www.shadesbeyondgray.com, *The Bottom Line, Amoret Online,* and the 'zine *Problem Child.* She has been interviewed on Playboy Radio and "SexLife Live." Her website is www.CatTailor.com,   email CatTailor@gmail.com.

JAMES WILLIAMS is the author of ...*But I Know What You Want.* His fiction has appeared widely in print and online publications and anthologies, including *Best American Erotica 1995, 2001,* and *2003,* all edited by Susie Bright; *Best Gay Erotica 2002, 2004,* and *2005,* all edited by Richard Labonté; and *Best SM Erotica* and *Best SM Erotica 2,* both edited by M. Christian. He made his nonfiction debut with "The Mother and Child Reunion" in *Walking Higher: Gay Men Write About the Deaths of Their Mothers,* edited by Alexander Renault. He was the subject of profile interviews in *Different Loving* and *Sex: An Oral History.* His slightly stagnant website can be found at www.jaswilliams.com.

ABOUT THE EDITOR

RICHARD LABONTÉ has been series editor of *Best Gay Erotica* since 1997. He writes a book review column, "Book Marks," for Q Syndicate, and a monthly newsletter about gay books, *Books To Watch Out For*. For a change of pace, he also edits writing about such subjects as IT management best practices and what's new about the natural gas pipeline infrastructure of Ontario. He lives in rural Perth and more-rural Calabogie, Ontario, with his husband Asa.